STOLEN SON

A GRIPPING PSYCHOLOGICAL THRILLER THAT WILL HAVE YOU HOOKED

COLE BAXTER

Illustrated by
NATASHA SNOW

Edited by
VALORIE CLIFTON

Copyright © 2018 by Cole Baxter

All rights reserved.

Cover design by Natasha Snow

Edited by Valorie Clifton

No part of this book may be reproduced in any form or by any electronic or mechanical means, including information storage and retrieval systems, without written permission from the author, except for the use of brief quotations in a book review.

This book is a work of fiction. Any resemblance to persons, living or dead, or places, events or locations is purely coincidental. The characters are all productions of the authors' imagination.

CONTENTS

Mailing List	v
Chapter 1	1
Chapter 2	13
Chapter 3	25
Chapter 4	35
Chapter 5	47
Chapter 6	59
Chapter 7	69
Chapter 8	79
Chapter 9	91
Chapter 10	101
Chapter 11	113
Chapter 12	125
Chapter 13	137
Chapter 14	147
Chapter 15	163
Chapter 16	175
Chapter 17	187
Chapter 18	199
Chapter 19	213
Chapter 20	225
Chapter 21	239
Chapter 22	253
Chapter 23	265
Chapter 24	275
Chapter 25	289
Chapter 26	299

Chapter 27	311
Chapter 28	325
About Cole Baxter	335
Also by Cole Baxter	337

Sign up for Cole's VIP Reader Club and find out about his latest releases, giveaways, and more. Click here!

Follow him on Facebook

CHAPTER ONE

My heart raced, Greg's fingers tangling through my thick hair as he kissed my body. Everything was perfect. His platinum hair reminded me of someone else. An uneasiness started to rise in my body, yet everything seemed so wonderful! I tried to let the pleasure of being with my husband consume me again. Nothing seemed to work. Something wasn't right, yet I couldn't place my finger on it. Begrudgingly, I shoved Greg away. I had to find our son, Gregory.

He glared at me as my pleasure turned to fear. His eyes, once as blue as the ocean itself, had changed. There was nothing but darkness in them. I tried to scream but the sound wouldn't escape my throat. All around me, the bedroom began to shake as pictures fell from the walls. Behind them, blood oozed out, thick and black like putrid sludge. Greg was gone, and the dark figure which replaced him triggered my fear and memory. He was the bad man, the one who liked to force his way with me.

Before his thick fingers could wrap around my throat, I screamed again, praying for anyone to hear me and come to my rescue but knowing it was already too late. I closed my eyes as his figure faded away. It wasn't until the menacing laughter stopped that I opened them again. A woman ran into my room, fear creasing her youthful face as she rushed to my side.

"Ms. Simmons! Are you in pain?" she yelled over my screams.

I nodded at first before the screaming stopped and turned to choked sobs. "It was just a bad dream. Oh, God!"

I took in my surroundings, the fear replaced by panic. It was as familiar as the dream had been to me. The stark white walls and subtle sounds of machines filled my senses. Harsh chemicals burned my nostrils as the memories came flooding back. I was in the hospital.

"Please," I gasped. "Please, not again! My son, where is my son?"

The nurse shook her head. "Ms. Simmons, you've suffered a pretty serious concussion."

I didn't care about what she was saying. The only thing that mattered was finding Gregory. I started to rip the needles and tape from my arms, much to the nurse's dismay. She tried to steady my hands, pulling them away from the IV that was in my arm. She was stronger than I gave her credit for, but I had something worth fighting for.

"You don't understand! I have to find Gregory. He is special. He has Asperger's and will be so scared! Where is my brother? Where is Tom?"

The nurse shifted her feet, looking around uneasily, and I knew something was wrong.

"Ms. Simmons, if you would just calm down, I can have the officer who was at the scene talk with you," she said. I jumped to interrupt but she raised an authoritative finger. "Otherwise, I'll have to bring in an orderly to hold you down. Then you'll get a nice sedative and we can try this again in a few hours."

I ground my teeth together. I had never been one for confrontation and this instance was no different. It took a great deal for me to get angry. The rage I felt inside was easy enough to pinpoint. I no longer thought that it was ten years ago when I'd just woken from the coma. Now I knew that something had happened, and my son was in danger.

"Fine," I hissed. "Go get the officer and make it quick. I want to know where my son is right now."

She glared at me but said nothing as she disappeared out the door again. I sat back, taking a deep breath and trying to focus on exactly what had happened. The details were still so sketchy. My memory was selective at best, one of the reasons I saw Dr. Andrews. Gloria was helping me to remember the sordid details of my kidnapping ten years ago. I closed my eyes, taking a deep breath and reaching for the past.

Tom, along with us and my mother, had all been decorating for Christmas. It was Gregory's favorite time of year. The bright colors and potential for new games always drove him wild. With his Asperger's, Christmas decorating was something he loved to do in a routine fashion. We had started with the tinsel, every strand delicately placed on our fake tree.

Some might have considered the task tedious, but not me. I saw the genius and order in everything that my nine-year-old did. My mother and brother loved him beyond words too. Something had happened then, a phone call. Even the memory made my heart race. My eyes darted to the ancient grandfather clock in the hall as it chimed six times. He always called at six.

Gregory's eyes met mine. I'd tried so hard to shelter him, but his gift made it a challenge. He could pick up on someone's emotional change before they ever knew it was going to happen. I watched his face fall for a split second before a hard mask replaced it. He turned back to his tinsel. I took a deep breath and went to the phone in the hallway.

"Hello?"

"You fucking whore," the disguised voice seethed. "I want my boy. I want the pup I gave to my bitch when I seeded you."

"The police are tracking this line, you bastard," I whispered with hateful anger.

He laughed, a menacing tone that I knew all too well. "Liar, liar, pants on fire. That's okay. My boy will know what you are soon enough."

"Don't you dare come near my son," I said quickly.

The line went dead. He never stayed on the phone long. Just enough to remind me that my rapist and Greg's killer was still out there. I slammed the phone down, my hands shaking with fear. From the living room, I saw Gregory jump and look back at me as he covered his ears. It was a rookie mistake on my part. He was so sensitive to sounds.

I smiled at him, trying to keep the sadness from my eyes. Tom appeared and started pulling out strands of tinsel to hand to Gregory. He was consumed once again by the project at hand. I took a deep breath and headed down the hall to the kitchen where Christmas carols and my mother's singing rang out. She smiled at me, pretending not to hear the phone ring.

"Why don't you run to the store with me? You need a little fresh air," she said with a grin.

I shook my head, still shaken. "No thanks. I'm going to take a hot shower. I don't really want to leave Gregory right now."

"I understand," she said softly, removing her flour-covered apron and setting it on the counter.

In a rare show of affection, she wrapped her arms around me. For the first time in a while, I let her hug me and returned the embrace. I felt comforted by her, though no one else was allowed to get so close to me. Of course, Gregory was the exception to that rule. She let me go and grabbed her purse from the hook near the back door.

"Let the boys know I'll be back soon, okay?"

"Sure," I said as I headed back into the living room.

"You okay?" Tom asked.

I shrugged. "I'm going to take a quick shower."

He nodded. "You always do."

"I'm sorry," I whispered. "His voice—"

"I know, you don't need to tell me. It makes you feel dirty all over again, but you know that I will keep you guys safe, right?"

I smiled at him and nodded. "You always do."

He laughed at the play on words as I headed up the steps in the hallway to the bathroom I shared with my mother. It wasn't ideal living with her, but I needed the help with Gregory. My part-time income as an app developer helped support the household. If I was being honest with myself, it wasn't just Gregory who needed the emotional support.

Even after ten years, I still woke in the middle of the night screaming. I softly shut the bathroom door, turning on the water and trying desperately to shake free from the memories. Why was I never able to remember my attacker? Frustration and anxiety washed over me as I tried desperately to force the memories away.

In the thick of the battle, I heard a scream. My eyes flew open, heart pounding as I tried to decipher whether it was real or once again my own screams as my attacker forced himself on me again in the memory. Just as I reached for the door, a gut-wrenching scream rang out in the small house, followed by Gregory's own blood-curdling scream for his uncle.

There was no more hesitation as I flew out the bathroom door and down the steps. Tom was lying on the floor, face down as blood trickled from a large wound to his back. I ran to him, my fingers desperately searching for a pulse as I reached for the phone. Gregory had to be safe. He had to have made it to our secret hiding spot.

My fingers frantically punched in the number for

the police as I quickly put pressure on my brother's wound.

"Emergency services," a woman answered.

"Please, someone has broken into my home. My brother was stabbed."

"Is the intruder still there?"

I swallowed against my dry throat. It hadn't even crossed my mind until that instance. Before I could think, before I could even process what she'd said, I heard footsteps behind me. I tried to turn around and lunge at whoever it was, but they were larger and much faster than I was. His burly fist, the same one as ten years before, connected with my cheek and sent me reeling to the ground. Darkness settled in, and the last thing I could recall was his kneeling down next to me, my son struggling in his grip.

"Told you I'd get my boy, bitch. I'll see you again real soon."

I SHUDDERED, my eyes flying open and bringing me back to the hospital room. I jumped when I saw a shadow standing in the corner. I was about to scream when Jacob stepped forward, his rotund belly and curly, carrot-colored hair ringing a note of familiarity in my mind. His eyes showed nothing but anger.

"Jacob?" I whispered. "What on earth are you doing here?"

"Where else do you think I would be? Annabeth, are you okay? They wouldn't tell me anything because I'm not family. I only got up here because of your mother."

I sighed. "No." The words wouldn't come to me. I couldn't admit it to him or even myself. "He stabbed Tom. No one in this place will tell me where he is or whether he made it."

Jacob's eyes widened in shock. "You know who it was?"

I nodded. "The same man who killed Greg. He has some hairbrained idea that my baby is his son."

"I guess for a madman, that's an easy assumption to make. I mean . . ." Jacob said awkwardly. "You were kidnapped on your honeymoon."

I glared at him. Jacob had been a friend of the family for the last fifteen years, but sometimes, he drove me mad. I tried not to hold his faults against him, like now. Admittedly, it was hard. I needed him to be a friend, not play the devil's advocate. Even as we spoke, his eyes softened into the puppy dog I knew him as. Jacob's feelings for me were no secret. He'd reminded me of them as recently as two days ago.

"Jacob, I know that Gregory is Greg's child," I told

him softly. It was the truth. All I needed to do was look in his eyes to know it was.

"But you never had his DNA tested."

"Please stop," I begged him. "I don't want to talk about that right now. Have you seen Tom? No one will tell me anything."

He softened, moving to the bed and sitting down carefully. "He's alive but his condition isn't great. He was stabbed in the spine. No one knows how he managed to pull through."

"He always was a fighter," I said as tears prickled my eyes.

"Annabeth," Jacob said carefully. "If you remember anything, you need to tell me now."

"I remember it all, just not what really matters. Who is Greg's killer?"

Jacob cleared his throat and took my hand, looking directly at me. My heart started to race with fear.

I shook my head. "No, Jacob, please. No."

"Annabeth," he whispered. "You already know what happened. It's Gregory."

I started to sob, dry heaving as the tears started to fall down onto my lap. "Oh, God. Say it."

"I'm so sorry, Annabeth, but Gregory is missing. The police believe that he was kidnapped by the same man who stabbed Tom."

"Greg's killer," I choked.

"Yes, the same. Do you remember anything about what happened? Did you get a look at his face?"

I scoffed. "Don't you think if I had seen his face, I'd be singing to the police right now?"

"Well," he muttered. "They are right outside, waiting to talk to you. I wouldn't let them in until you were ready though."

Smiling at Jacob, I pulled my hand away and sat up in the bed. "I think I'm ready. Would you mind sending them in when you leave?"

"You don't want me here with you?"

I shook my head. "Not this time. But thank you for everything."

Jacob nodded. I could see the hurt in his eyes, but there was no time to placate his feelings. My son was missing, and I was going to get him back.

CHAPTER TWO

Jacob turned away from the door, noticing the tears springing to my eyes again. I sucked in a breath and tried to get myself under control. For a man as large as he was, Jacob crossed the room quickly and was once again at my bed.

"I'm fine," I said. "Really."

He shook his head and wrapped his arms around me. The touch was unwelcomed and I instantly tensed. Instinctively, I shoved him away from me with a little more force than intended and he went stumbling back. His face flushed a deep red as he brushed himself off.

"I'm sorry, Jacob. I don't like being touched," I said in a tone so firm, it shocked me. "You know that. I've never been okay with anyone touching me."

"God," he snapped. "I thought we were past that, Annabeth. I was just trying to comfort you."

"I know you were," I said through gritted teeth.

"I have been nothing but patient and understanding with you. A lesser man would find someone who cared back."

"Jacob, I've told you I don't feel that way."

"Save it," he snapped.

Jacob jerked the door open, storming out of the room. His temper had always been short, though most of the time, he tried to hide it from me. It was surprising to see him on edge, especially since I was the one with a missing son. I didn't have time to mull over his attitude before a handsome man in a police uniform stepped into the room.

He took one look at my frantic gaze and stepped away from the door, leaving it open, to my approval and surprise. Extending a hand, he slowly walked forward. Each step seemed carefully calculated. Suddenly, I felt very frumpy. I had to look like a hot mess, but it didn't matter. If Officer Stud Muffin was going to help me find my baby boy, then I'd work with him.

"Ms. Simmons?" he asked. "I'm Detective Reyes. How are you feeling?"

"Angry," I snapped quicker than expected. "I want to know what you are doing to find my son."

He smiled sympathetically. "I can't imagine what you're going through right now. We are doing everything possible to find Gregory. Is there anything you can tell me about your attacker?"

I cringed. "Yes. It was the same man as before. The one who killed my Greg."

Reyes looked down at his notepad and flipped a few pages back. "I'm sorry for your loss. That was ten years ago, correct?"

"Yes," I whispered.

"You were in a coma?"

"For twenty-six days," I said.

"What happened after that?"

"Doesn't your notebook tell you all that? I lost everything from amnesia."

"That's rough. How is your memory doing now?"

I shrugged. "Some days are better than others. It took me years to remember everything that happened before the attack."

"But you do remember it all now?"

Shaking my head, I tried again to recall what had happened on that fateful night. My body shook, my head starting to hurt instantly. I was used to the pain. "Mostly, everything right up to the attack. The rest is still in bits and pieces. I don't know who attacked me, if that's what you're asking. All I know is that it was the same man."

"How can you be sure?" Reyes asked.

I glared at him. "Because you remember the person who had his way with you repeatedly. You remember their smell, the shape of their body, everything but what the police need to catch him. When someone spends a month shoving their dick, fist, and anything else they find lying around inside your body, you can't forget." My voice cracked. "No matter how hard you try."

His eyes grew wide, a red blush gracing his cheeks as he quickly looked away from me and back down to the notebook. "Um."

Taking a deep breath, I closed my eyes. "Listen, if you aren't going to help me find my baby, then go away. I can do it without you."

"Annabeth," he said softly. "I really want to help you, but we just don't have a lot to go on. Is there anything else at all that you can tell me? Eye color, hair?"

"No!" I yelled, my temper finally breaking through. "I've told you everything! Why don't you send the nurse in here so she can get me out of this place on your way out, okay?"

Reyes raised his hands in a show of surrender, taking a step back while I calmed down. His eyes shifted briefly to the door, but instead of leaving, he waited. All I wanted was for him to go away. I wanted time to collect my thoughts and try to get a plan together. If I couldn't count on the police, I would take care of it myself. Reyes didn't seem to understand just how dire the situation really was.

"I'm sorry I upset you," he said after a while. "I can't imagine how I would feel if one of my girls went missing. You are handling all of this much better than I would."

My eyes lifted in surprise. "You have kids?"

He nodded. "Two girls. Their mother passed away three years ago."

"Oh, my God. I'm so sorry. I didn't know."

"It's okay. There was no way for you to know. I don't really share details of my life on cases, but it seemed like you needed to know."

"Thank you," I said. "How old are they?"

A sly grin passed his lips. "Twin girls, seven. They certainly give me a run for my money. Your son has Asperger's, correct?"

I nodded. "He's high-functioning though. Only certain things set him off, like loud noises. He's so smart though. I had to hire a tutor for myself just to keep up with him. He loves puzzles."

"Maybe that's a good thing then. Perhaps he'll be able to find a way to escape the kidnapper."

"I wish I could have the same faith as you, but I've been there before, wherever the man held me.

It's a maze. I don't even know if we were in a building."

"You told the nurse the last time you were here that it smelled damp? Perhaps a basement?"

I shuddered. "I just don't know. All I can think about is finding him. I feel so useless sitting here, doing nothing."

"But you aren't doing nothing," Reyes said as he carefully took a step closer to me. "The more details that I have about the man who took him and what you went through last time, the better my chances are of being able to catch him."

"You want to know about the last time?" I asked.

My heart started to race. The idea of reliving the past wasn't something I took lightly. I'd spent years trying to keep things bottled up inside. I knew it wasn't healthy to keep things in. My doctor had said as much several times. But opening up to a complete stranger? That was almost more than I could take altogether. Why would I tell him the sordid details of my capture? I shuddered and closed my eyes, softly shaking my head.

"Annabeth, how am I going to find your son unless you can help me?" he pressed. "Do it for your boy, not for me or anyone else. Help me find him, please."

I took a deep breath, shuddering at the memory as I cleared my throat. "Some of it, I remember like it was yesterday. Some details still come and go. I can't count on them. Most of the time, I wonder if I can even count on myself."

I looked up at him and chuckled. "You might want to pull up a chair. This is going to take a little bit of time."

He grinned, quickly grabbing a chair from the corner of the room and pulling it close to the bed. "I have all the time in the world."

"But Gregory might not," I whispered.

When he reached across the bed and gently took my hand, I winced and pulled away. The shocking realization that his touch didn't send me running for the door wasn't something I could think about. I had to be strong for my son. I'd already faced down the monster, but now he had my boy. I had to stay focused, no matter how painful it was.

"It's strange," I whispered. "Even the simplest things like the color of my attacker's eyes elude me at times, but not Greg. Everything about him is crystal clear."

"Did you lose any memories of him when you woke up last time?"

I nodded my head. "It's very disconcerting to wake up and not be sure of who you are. My mother would sit at my side for hours and show me pictures, hoping to jog some recollection. Listening to her and hearing the heartbreak in her voice were almost unbearable. Slowly, pieces of it started to come back, but I still didn't recognize the carefree, young, and happy woman I saw in the pictures. It was only when she showed me Gregory's photo that I started to remember him."

"Then," I stammered, "Then, she told me what happened. How they had found his body in the cabin that we were renting for our honeymoon."

"You were married young," Reyes pressed.

"Very. Nineteen. But my mother loved Gregory like her own son. He was just a few years older than me, but our love was the kind you find in a fairytale. We met in school as children and grew up together. When we announced our engagement, my mother wasn't even surprised. She loved him almost as much as I did."

"What about his family?"

"He never really had one. His older brother took care of him, but he was just a kid himself, to be honest. By the time Gregory was eighteen, he was living with my mother and me. He went right to college and still worked to help her pay bills. We were just kids, of course, and broke up a time or two. But our love was stronger than the outside world, and we always seemed to find each other again."

"That's beautiful," he whispered.

I chucked. "It's tragic. I never wanted a story like

Romeo and Juliet. We had a simple wedding, neither of us having much family. Just my mom, my brother, and Jacob."

Reyes's eyebrows lifted. "You've known Mr. Morse that long?"

I nodded. "He did some work for my mother when I was a teen. I guess we sort of adopted him into the family after that."

"That's very admirable of her."

I shrugged. "I never really thought much of it. He needed a family and we had the room. I think people see him and think the worst. He's harmless, really. He's just got a short fuse sometimes."

"Very little respect for authority too, it would seem."

I cocked my head. "I've never seen that side of him."

Reyes shook his head, a somewhat fake smile appearing. "Please, continue with your story. I don't want to get off track."

I frowned but dropped the subject. If he was going to help me find Gregory, I had to stay focused. Getting sidetracked talking about Jacob wasn't going to help anyone.

"Um," I muttered. "Right. So, we were married. My mother paid for us to get a cabin in the Catskills for a weekend. He was working, and I was finishing up college, so it was just for a few nights." I sighed as I recalled the memory. "That was all we needed though. Just a little time for us to really be a married couple."

"You were still living with your mother at that point?" he asked.

"Yeah, but she didn't mind us even then. It wasn't supposed to be our forever home. We'd been saving for months to rent our own place. The proudest moment of our lives was the day we signed the lease. I was going to tell my mother when we got back from our honeymoon."

I swallowed as I continued. "The first night there was wonderful. The next day, I left just for a few minutes to go down to the store. We'd drunk our way through a bottle of wine and had every intention of doing the same that evening. It was raining, and the roads were slick."

The memories were overpowering. I blinked back the tears. The closer we got to the kidnapping and later, the torture, the more I felt myself becoming unhinged. I knew from my sessions with Dr. Andrews that I had to breathe. If I didn't, then I would have a panic attack for certain, and I'd be no closer to the answers Reyes and I both needed. I glanced at him beneath my eyelashes. He sat, waiting so patiently for me to tell him more. Where was he ten years ago when my husband's murder had gone unsolved?

"Are you okay?" he asked softly.

"Yeah," I croaked. "I haven't shared this with anyone besides my doctor. It's just going to take me a little time."

"I understand," Reyes said as he sat back.

"So, the road getting to the cabin was a mess. The mud was one of the first memories that came back to me. Everything was washed out. When I got back to the cabin, I saw tracks in the mud. It was one of those things that I just didn't think about until it was too late. I thought maybe the cabin was up high enough that my tracks hadn't been washed out. There was no car waiting for me, nothing. I think back to that moment and wonder if I had been more cautious, more vigilant, maybe things would be different."

"Hey," he whispered. "You can't be doing that to yourself. You couldn't know what would be waiting for you."

"Or who," I gasped.

All at once, it came flooding back to me. I started to shake.

"Annabeth?" His voice sounded far away.

"I can't!" My chest hurt. I closed down, giving up my life up to the darkness.

CHAPTER THREE

"Annabeth?" Reyes whispered. "Hey, do I need to get the nurse?"

I swallowed as everything came back into focus. I hadn't had a blackout in so long that it caught me off guard. Whenever they came, new memories followed close behind. I wasn't sure if I wanted them, even though they slowly filled in the blanks that were missing.

"No," I croaked. "I don't want that woman back in here. Just give me a second."

He nodded his head in understanding as he sat back against the chair. I was grateful for the space. The room always felt like it was closing in around me for some time after an attack. The air felt thick, heavier than it should. I sucked in a sharp breath as the first memory came back to me. It wasn't much but it was enough to knock me off kilter.

"It was muddy," I whispered.

"Outside?" Reyes pressed gently.

I shook my head vigorously. He wasn't understanding me and that made sense. My words were barely comprehensible as the memory flooded back. I looked down at my fingers. Though they were clean, I knew that they had once been covered in mud. Gritty mud that had been sitting in the room for some time. It made my skin feel thick, crackling underneath the pressure as I rubbed them together. Plus, it had a strong, pungent smell to it. Like rotting oil.

"There was mud wherever I was being held. Moisture on a dirt floor," I told him, still looking down at my fingers.

"So, like a basement?" Reyes asked.

"I don't know. It would make sense with the smell. But the mud, they should have tested it when I was free. I know that it was still there when I left."

"I can find out if they kept the evidence at the precinct," he said quickly as he pulled out his phone.

"Not right now," I whispered to him. "If I don't get this out of me now, I can't be sure that I will ever have the courage to share it with you again."

Instantly, he slipped his phone back into his pocket and gave me his undivided attention. It was nice to have someone there who really cared. But it reminded me of my other commitments.

"How bad off is my brother?" I asked.

He shook his head. "The knife nicked his spine. You are the only reason he is alive. Calling 911 was crucial."

"He isn't awake?"

"No, they have him in a medically induced coma. Any movement on his part could sever the nerves and leave him paralyzed for life. They are hoping to get him into surgery before they wake him up, but they can't even do that until his condition has stabilized a little bit. Do you want me to go get your mother? I know the doctors told her you were awake."

I winced. "I think that she wants to be with my brother. I can't believe this is happening. If anything happens to Tom, my mother will never forgive me."

"You saved his life," Reyes reminded me.

"It wouldn't have been in danger if that maniac wasn't obsessed with me to begin with."

"Don't blame yourself," he whispered before flipping through his notebook. "Do you feel like you are ready to continue?"

I ground my teeth. The only way I was going to get through things was by pressing forward. I nodded, ready to face my demons once again.

"The first sign that something was off was the door.

It was open. The mountains were brisk, and Greg had been stocking the fireplace when I left, so at first, I thought maybe it was just too much heat and he'd cracked it open. I called for him when I went in but there was that damn mud again. The tracks were too big for Greg. My heart was beating so loudly I couldn't even hear my own thoughts. I went around the corner to the kitchen, wondering if we had a guest."

"Why would you think that?"

"Because the owner mentioned he was going to stop by at some point to add chemicals to the hot tub. He was an older man, super friendly."

"But it wasn't him, was it?" Reyes whispered.

I sobbed, my body trembling as I shook my head. "No, it was my Greg. He—" I choked. "He was just lying there on the ground. He wasn't moving and there was blood everywhere. The bag fell from my hands and glass shattered. The wine, it splashed into . . . into his blood."

"Hey," Reyes said, quickly cutting me off. "We don't need to get into all that, okay? Just skip to what happened next. You don't need to be going through it all again. I can find out the details some other way."

I nodded my head vigorously, thankful for his sensitivity on the subject. "After I got back to my feet, I heard someone approaching me from behind. I spun around, but by that time, the man was already right behind me. I didn't even have time to scream before he pressed a rag to my mouth. The doctors said they thought it was chloroform from how I felt. Everything went dark after that until I woke up in that place."

"You called it a maze?" he asked. "Is that right?"

"Yes and no. That's the closest I could think of it, but in reality, it was probably just a few locked doors. Either way, I couldn't find my way out, at least not for a while."

"You were missing for over a month?"

"That sounds about right."

"It sounds like your son surviving in your womb was a miracle."

I smiled, thinking of my boy. "He always was a fighter."

"Then he will keep fighting now. Everything you've told me is incredibly helpful. I'd like to get out there and start looking for this monster. Every second counts when a child is missing."

"Thank you," I whispered.

As Reyes stood and held out his hand, I shook it firmly. I'd never claimed to be a good judge of character, but something told me that I could count on him to do what it would take to find Gregory. A weight had been lifted from my own table.

"Do you know if my mother has been by?" I asked

him as he handed me a business card. I grabbed my phone and quickly took a picture of it.

Thanks to my background in phone apps, I knew that the safest place for it was going to be stored in one of the many programs I had personally developed years ago. It had sold for a small fortune. It, along with a few others, had sufficiently set Gregory and myself up with enough money to live on modestly, though I still worked a little to give us some spending money.

He looked sheepishly at the door and I knew the answer. "No, sorry. She was pretty wrapped up with your brother when I questioned her."

"Right," I muttered. "I guess that makes sense. She will probably be up before too long. Have you heard anything about when they're letting me get out of here? I want to be of some help to you."

"I heard them talking about tomorrow, but you have to do what they say, okay? I promise I will keep you updated with whatever we find out."

Before I could thank him once again, a familiar but increasingly loud voice came from the hallway. I cringed, knowing it was Jacob at once. Glancing at the clock, I saw that the detective and I had spent almost an hour together behind closed doors. The last time I'd been alone with a man that long was when my attacker visited me before my escape. It solidified my growing feelings for the understanding detective even more.

"You think you have a right to leave a frail woman alone with a man for that long?" Jacob yelled from the hallway.

Reyes looked back at me as he opened the door. "Mr. Morse? I was just finishing up with Annabeth. Perhaps we can go somewhere quiet. I have a few follow-up questions for you as well."

Jacob's gaze shot to me. "I am comfortable talking about anything in front of Annabeth. What are friends for if they can't stick by you?"

My jaw tightened. I knew that he was upset with me for making him leave the room, but I didn't want to focus on it. I was short on friends and family anymore. What good would it do to upset one of the few still sticking by my side?

"It's fine, Jacob. I'm just going to take a little nap anyway," I lied.

"You do seem to have a very special interest in everything with the case. As a matter of fact, you were trying to get one of my men to give you details that aren't to be released to anyone outside of the victim's family."

Jacob's face flushed a deep red, the rage evident just below the tense surface of his oily skin. "I have a right to look out for Annabeth. She doesn't have anyone else around here. Have you seen anyone?"

Reyes, to my surprise, seemed angered by Jacob.

"Are you in an intimate relationship with Ms. Simmons?"

"What?" I stammered, interjecting before Jacob could speak. "Of course we are not in an intimate relationship!"

"Annabeth," Reyes said, carefully turning back to me and once again cutting an enraged Jacob from the conversation, "I didn't mean to cause you any more stress. Sometimes, I have to asked questions that don't make much sense. Would you like us to leave?"

"No," I said softly.

"I think that would be best," Jacob said suddenly. "As a matter of fact, I think that you have been through enough. I think I should handle the police from here on out. It's obvious that they are stressing you out even more."

I glared at Jacob. "My son is the one missing. I am not some frail damsel in distress, Jacob. I can take care of myself."

His passive smile only served to anger me more as he spoke softly, like he was trying to appease a child's tantrum. "Of course, you can." Jacob turned back to Reyes. "Let's go get this over with."

Reyes rolled his eyes but shot me a sly grin. "You have my card if you need anything, okay? Don't hesitate to call me anytime, day or night, if you think of anything that might help the case."

"You promise you will tell me if you find anything?" I whispered to him.

"I give you my word as an officer and as a parent."

I nodded my head, ignoring the look of anger on Jacob's face as Reyes stepped from the room. All I wanted was a little time by myself to really process everything that was happening. I also wanted to see my mother. From what I'd been told, the only visitor I'd had during my stay was Jacob. Even if he could be brash at times, I couldn't lose the only friend I had.

"I'll be back to talk in a little bit, okay?" Jacob said softly. "Just let me handle this clown first. Is there anything that you need?"

I shuddered. "I just want my son back." It was all I could think of. "Just find him and bring him back to me. He's already lost a father he never knew, and I've lost the only man I'll ever love. Bring him back to me."

"Don't say you'll never love again," Jacob said, his congested tone like nails on a chalkboard. "You will always have me."

"I know, but I don't see you like that," I whispered to him as a reminder. "You know that I will never love you in that way. But you are such a wonderful friend."

He said nothing in reply, and for that I was grateful. I couldn't handle any more of his drama. As if losing everything wasn't enough, I was still reeling over what Reyes had told me. My own mother hadn't made the effort to come and see me. She did blame me for what Tom was going through. It was worse that I couldn't find anything else out about my brother. If he died, it would be yet another death that I was responsible for.

My attacker's words haunted me as I tried desperately to shake them from my mind. His thick breath, stinking of alcohol, was just as strong as the day I first smelled it. Chapped lips scratched at my tender skin as he whispered into my ear.

'You are the reason he's dead, bitch. You just couldn't keep your legs closed. I hope you know that you will always have your worthless husband's blood on your head. I'm gonna hurt you so much that you'll wish you'd never met that useless piece of shit.'

"No," I said to the empty room. I squeezed my eyes shut. "No! It wasn't my fault!"

CHAPTER FOUR

"His hands are around my neck. I can feel them," I choked.

"That's okay," Gloria softly pressed. "How far around your neck do they go? Can you tell me?"

"No." I swallowed back against the dryness in my mouth. "He's choking me, I—" I gasped. "I just have to keep fighting. It hurts! Everything hurts."

"Okay, Annabeth, I want you to come back to me now, okay?"

"Stop," I whispered.

Images of my life after the kidnapping flashed in front of me between the searing pain of my memories. I had to remember the details. I had to know everything that could help them find out who took my boy.

"They are big, his hands," I said quickly. "And rough, always so rough. The calluses dig into my neck."

"Can you smell anything?" she asked.

Something pungent filled my nose, jolting me out of the trance and back into the hospital room. Instantly, my cheeks flushed red as I recalled what the smell was.

"He, um . . . he liked to urinate after he was done with me."

"Oh," Gloria said softly. "I think that we've done enough for now. You have made some big strides today. I don't want to push much further and risk a breakdown. Have you heard anything from the police?"

I shook my head. "No, but, um, the detective on the case seems to know what he's doing. He has children himself."

"Really?" she said, her eyebrows raising.

I blushed. "It's nothing like that. I have confidence that he is going to find Gregory."

"You haven't spoken so highly of a man besides Greg in the ten years we've been working together. That's something I would like to explore later on at some point."

"Okay," I agreed, knowing that compromise was key to our relationship. "But not right now."

"That's understandable," she said. "I think we need to go back to the man who took Gregory. You are sure that it's the same man."

"Why else would he come for him? He's sick. He thinks my baby is somehow his. I don't understand it. I was pregnant already. And look at Gregory. You can't deny that he is Greg's."

She smiled affectionately. "I know. He looks just like him. Even his build is the same. But wouldn't it be easier to get a DNA test and close this down once and for all?"

"It doesn't matter to me," I snapped quickly.

"Your captor, though, the man you believe took your son, has some attachment to him. It might help the case if you took a DNA test."

"I don't want to, okay?" I shuddered.

In my heart and mind, I knew that Gregory was Greg's child. His namesake shared so many of his father's features that it was often like I was looking into a memory from my past where Greg was a young man. My heart was pounding. What if I was wrong? What if somehow, the results came back and showed that Gregory was the offspring of my rapist? Shuddering, I shook my head once again.

"No, it's not possible. We have to find a different way to get him back. I just have to keep pushing myself. The memories will come to me. Something will help us to catch him."

She patted my leg soothingly. It was nice to have

her there. Her eyes darted to the clock and I knew that our time together was almost up.

"Please, Doctor," I whispered. "Please just let me go under one more time. There has to be something of importance that I'm forgetting."

"And you will find it, okay? We don't want to break down those walls though. Remember what we talked about? Your mind is protecting you from what happened. If he smashes through that wall, I can't be sure of your ability to cope with it all at once."

"But think about Gregory," I blurted out, the tears now flowing down my cheeks. "I can't imagine how scared he must be."

"Tomorrow, I will come back here, okay? We can try again, but for now, you need to rest."

I nodded in agreement, though it wasn't what I really wanted. "Have you seen my mother?"

Gloria nodded softly. I could always count on her to tell me the truth no matter how painful it was. "I did stop in and see her. She is dealing with a lot of pain right now. Don't let her feelings weigh too heavily on you, okay? I know that you feel guilty, but you need to shake that off."

"Tom was stabbed because of me," I reminded her. "How am I supposed to not feel guilty about that?"

"Tom was stabbed because a maniac is obsessed with you. That is not your fault."

"How did he find us? Why did he find us? What's his obsession with me and my son?"

"Those are all very good questions, and once they catch him, I'm sure that you will get the answers you are looking for. But you know that I don't have them. All I can do is help you to unlock the pieces of your past that are missing."

"Which you won't do," I grumbled.

She chuckled softly. "Now, now, you know that we can't rush this sort of thing. Just give it time."

A soft rapping at the door made me look up quickly. My heart raced at the possibility of Reyes returning so soon to give me an update. When my lumbering friend's head poked through the door, I smiled at Jacob. He'd apologized for being so protective over me, and I easily forgave him. I needed someone reliable like him in my life. Gloria bristled at the sight of him but said nothing, smiling politely as she rose.

"I will see you tomorrow, Annabeth. Try and get some sleep tonight, okay?" Her eyes darted back to Jacob. "Don't let anyone keep you from taking care of your needs."

"I won't. I'm just going to wait up a little while longer and see if my mom makes it up. I know she's worried about Gregory and Tom."

"She will be up. I'm sure of it," Gloria said in her comforting tone.

Jacob cleared his throat and Gloria shot him a look that could kill before slipping out the door. I wasn't thrilled about his coming back. My mind had gone over details that I hadn't had to think about in a very long time. I could at least stay awake long enough to spend a few minutes with Jacob, though, especially knowing that he'd been down to see my brother.

"How is Tom doing?" I asked.

He sat in the chair that Gloria had left behind. I didn't like how close he was to me. His massive weight brushed against the bed, dangerously close to my legs. Fighting the urge to tell him to move, I scooted my body away a little. The move didn't go unnoticed by him, though he didn't say anything about it. Some things weren't ever going to change.

"He's holding on, thank God," Jacob said. "I can't imagine what you must be going through."

"No." I winced. "I wouldn't wish this on my worst enemy. Thankfully, detective Reyes seems more than capable of handling the situation."

"Reyes?" Jacob snorted. "That joke?"

"I don't think that he's a joke," I snapped back.

I'd been holding his card in my hand during the session with Dr. Andrews. It brought me comfort as I flicked it between my fingers. The edges were slightly worn down from constantly folding them back and forth. I let my mind wander a little bit as Jacob fell silent. He saw the card in my hand and instantly bristled.

Before I could react, Jacob snatched the card from my hand. Instantly, I pulled away from him, glaring at him. "What the hell?"

His eyes grew wide at my language. "Wow, I just wanted to look at it. I don't think it was right of him to put this kind of pressure on you."

"Pressure? It's just a business card, and I think it was nice of him to be so worried."

"You actually like that little snot? He was rude to me, tried to intimidate me with his questions."

"What kind of questions?" I asked him.

He rolled his eyes and shook his eye, "Nothing that you need to worry about. I think that I should handle the police from now on though. It's obviously too distressing for you."

I frowned. Reyes hadn't stressed me out at all. In fact, he was more soothing to me than I cared to admit to Jacob or anyone else. I shook my head softly.

"I don't think I need you to take care of them for me. But thank you for offering. I want to work with the detective. He seems so sure that he can help me find Gregory."

"Junior will be fine," Jacob said, doing his best to comfort me.

"Gloria thinks that I should do a DNA test," I said

softly. It wasn't that I wanted to share the details with Jacob, but I had no one else to talk with about it.

His eyes lit up a little at the break in the case. He'd been trying to push me to do a DNA test for years. I couldn't understand his obsession with it, but then again, Greg hadn't really been his favorite person. Knowing that Gregory wasn't really Greg's son would probably give him some strange justification in the matter. Even now, he had to assert that he was right about the situation.

"Finally, something we can agree on. When are you doing it?" he spat out, practically jumping from his seat.

I rolled my eyes at him. "I'm not going to do it. There is no need. She even admitted that Gregory is Greg's son beyond a shadow of a doubt. You know Gregory and you knew Greg. There is no denying his blood. We just have to find the sicko who thinks they have some claim to him." I tried to grab the business card again, but he jerked his massive body away from me. "Just give it back to me, okay?" I snapped.

He shook his head. "This isn't you, Annabeth. You aren't this grabby, rude woman I see now. You are kind to a fault. You've always been that way, though," he reminded me.

"Please just give it back, Jacob. Detective Reyes is

the first man I've met in a long time who doesn't look at me like I'm damaged goods."

"What about me?" he whined.

I chuckled softly. "You have never looked at me in that way. You've always been such a good friend. Especially now with Gregory missing. I just know that Reyes will be able to find him."

"Jesus, Annabeth, he's a cop, not a god," he said in a sharp tone.

"Fine," I said with a sigh. "You can keep the card."

"It's nice to see that you are finally letting some good sense get into that brain of yours. I will deal with him and the other police officers. You just need to focus on getting yourself better."

"I don't need you to protect me, Jacob," I hissed.

His face turned a deep red. I instantly regretted the harsh words. Before I could stop him or even reach out in a rare show of affection, Jacob was on his feet, pacing near the door.

"You know, I don't have to be here!" he blurted out at me. "I don't have to be sitting here taking this from you. All I've done is try to help you, and I can't even touch you, but this joke with a badge comes along and suddenly, I am chopped liver."

I shuddered in fear, his words so harsh. "Jacob, I'm sorry. You really have been an amazing friend. It's not like that—"

"Right," he interrupted. "I'm such a great friend. Would someone who's just a friend be here with you for two goddamn days? Would they be fielding every officer and question that the doctors have for you?"

"I know," I said, my throat dry. "I'm sorry. Please, just come sit back down."

"No!" he said, his tone cold. "You don't need me to protect you, remember?"

"I shouldn't have said that. I'm just so worried about Gregory."

He sighed, his temper cooling as he sat back down in the chair. His hand slid up the bed, resting next to my leg but not touching it. He was right on the fence of my comfort zone, but I didn't move. My body was frozen. I didn't want to risk pushing him away again. Then I would be entirely alone.

"I just want you to trust me, Annabeth. After everything that we have been through together, just a little bit of trust."

I nodded without thinking. "You are absolutely right. You can keep the business card. I shouldn't have tried to handle it all myself anyway. I'm just so worried."

"And the DNA test?" he pressed.

I closed my eyes and tried to think about what Gloria had taught me. I had to come to grips with these decisions on my own, without letting others influence me. If I told Jacob that, though, I knew he would be upset all over again.

"I promise that I will think about it, okay?"

"Fine," he grumbled.

I watched him slip Detective Reyes's card into his wallet and noted that he already had several other cards in there. It was a small thing to give him if it meant keeping him happy. After all, I'd already put Reyes's information into my phone.

CHAPTER FIVE

"Okay, Annabeth, everything looks good. You are ready to be discharged," the nurse said as she read over her clipboard. "It looks like we've released you into your mother's care for now. The doctor doesn't want you driving for a few days. She should be up here soon to get you if you want to get dressed."

"Thank you," I said, still in shock that Mom would be the one to take me home. "Do you know how my brother is doing?'

She smiled softly. "He's a fighter, that's for sure. His condition is still not great, but he's a little more stable. Every day that he keeps fighting is another win for us."

"That's good to hear," I said in a hushed whisper. "Do you know if I can go down and see him?"

The nurse shook her head. "I don't think that would be a good idea. Dr. Andrews seemed to think it would stress you out more."

My cheeks blushed. "She spoke to you about me?"

Instantly, her eyes widened in apology. "I hope you don't mind. I didn't think you'd want the doctor to know that you were her patient, but I've worked with her in the past for my own issues. She really is wonderful."

"Agreed," I said with a breath of relief. "Okay, well I guess I'll just wait on my mother then."

The woman nodded and left me alone, my clothing folded up at the end of the bed. It didn't matter that my physical wounds had since healed. The emotional ones were bad enough that I felt like a cripple as I climbed from the bed and started to get dressed. My body was pale and thin, too thin for me to appreciate. I'd barely eaten since arriving at the hospital, my nerves too shot to consider a meal.

After I was dressed, I sat perched on the end of the bed for some time. What felt like an hour was probably only a quarter of one. My heart ached every time I thought about Gregory and what he must be enduring. Was he even still alive? I shuddered and tried to shake the morbid thoughts from my mind.

Reyes had been sure that the kidnapper wouldn't hurt him, at least not deathly. He wanted to keep Gregory as his own. Still, he didn't know Gregory like I did. A sensory overload could send him into a complete meltdown. Someone who didn't know him wouldn't be prepared to handle something like that. What if he got upset and the killer lost his temper? He was such a sweet boy.

I couldn't lose myself in the pain though. My mother walked in just as I felt my sanity slipping away. I quickly gathered my things and smiled at her. Her look was cold and calculating. A chip on her shoulder was evident. She didn't want to be there any more than I did, but I had the sneaking suspicion that I was the reason for her hostility.

"Thank you for coming to get me," I said softly.

"I didn't have any choice. There is nothing more I can do for Tom, and I still have a job I need to get back to."

"Oh," I said as my voice trailed off. I didn't want to know if she would have come for me if work didn't need her. The answer would probably bring more pain.

She rolled her eyes. "Listen, it's a shitty situation all around, okay? Can we please just get out of here? I've already missed two days of work. I don't want to be late on top of everything else."

"Sure," I muttered.

I quickly grabbed what few things I had and shuffled out the door. No one seemed to be looking in our direction, which I was grateful for. What was the point, anyway? People got stabbed and kids went missing all the time. It was just the world that we lived in anymore. We made our way down to her waiting car. I was careful to keep my eyes on the road and not strike up a conversation. She obviously didn't want one.

"How's Tom?" I whispered as we pulled into the driveway.

"Barely holding on. That's what happens when you get stabbed in the back by a psycho," she snapped.

"The police are doing everything they can," I reminded her.

"Right, because they did so much good when you went missing. Those dumbasses would still be spouting off about 'no leads' if you hadn't broken out. Gregory is just a kid, though." Her voice cracked. "And Tom."

I reached across the console and took her hand. "He is a fighter. Everyone is saying so. He will pull through this and we will find Gregory."

"I don't think I could forgive myself if he doesn't make it."

She'd left out her concern for Gregory's safe return. I knew that she was hurting and projecting that onto me. Why wouldn't she? I was the reason all of this had happened. I stepped out of the car and unlocked the front door without saying anything else to her. I couldn't handle the weight of my own guilt and sorrow along with the anger that she had toward me. If I could just find Gregory, then everything could go back to normal.

"You have a little time before work. Do you want to come in and I'll make some coffee?" I asked her as I set down my bag.

She shook her head. "I don't think so. I want to get there early. I might stop back by the hospital too."

I folded my hands in my lap. "I'd really like to talk to you about all of this. You were pretty quiet on the way over here."

"Look, Annabeth," she said quickly. "I love you and your brother so much, and Gregory has been a blessing. But . . ." I could hear the catch in her throat. "Right now, I just need a little bit of space, okay? Please, just let me go to work."

My back stiffened. It felt like eyes were watching me. I didn't want to be left alone, but how could I ask my mother to stay when she obviously needed her time away from me?

"Fine," I said quickly. "Then have a great day at work. Please let me know if there is any change in Tom's condition."

"I will," she said, her tone full of pain.

I knew that this wasn't easy for her. My own depression was constantly lingering in the back of my mind. I reached for the door, climbing out with shaking hands and slamming it behind me. I didn't wait to see her pull away. All I wanted to do was get inside the safety of our home. In that moment, I was very grateful for the new security system my mother had installed.

I quickly typed in the password and slipped inside, rearming it at once. It did little to ease my fear. The house was still too bright. If I could look out every window, then anyone could be looking in. Jogging through the house, I grabbed at the blinds and cords holding back curtains. I couldn't stop until the entire house was dark. Only the pale artificial lights that hung from the ceiling illuminated the house.

When I finally collapsed on the couch, my mind was racing. It was like the early days of my return from the kidnapping all over again. Every creaking board and dripping faucet sent my heart into a racing tailspin. I closed my eyes, thinking back to what Gloria had taught me. Deep breaths, counting backward from ten, until the room stopped spinning and I could breathe again.

Just as I was starting to calm down, the phone rang, and I jumped from the couch. I crept over to it, unsure whether it was my stalker. He never left a message.

Ring after ring, I held my breath. Finally, after what felt like eons, the machine picked up.

"Hi, Annabeth," said Detective Reyes.

My heart leapt and I scrambled to answer the phone. "Gabriel? Sorry, Detective Reyes?"

"Annabeth! I wasn't sure if you were home. Is everything okay?"

"Um, yes. Everything is fine. Why do you ask?"

"Well," he murmured shyly, "to be honest, I was just keeping an eye on your alarm. You know, just to make sure you made it home okay. It looked like you were running through the house pretty fast, from the motion sensors."

"You were watching me?" I blurted out. My fist hit my palm the second I said the words.

"Yeah, I guess I was. I'm sorry. I didn't mean to freak you out. I was just worried."

"That's okay," I said. "I'm fine, though, just adjusting to being in the house alone."

"Your mother isn't there with you?" he asked.

I cringed. It was an innocent enough question but still, it struck me wrong. I didn't want him or anyone else to know that I was alone. I knew it was impossible for him to be mine and Gregory's abductor. After all, Reyes was new to our police force for the most part, and he'd been nothing but kind.

"It's fine," I said softly. "She just ran out for a

second. Thank you for calling to check on me. Do you have any new leads on the case?"

"One," he said in an uncertain tone. "But I wouldn't even call it a lead yet. As soon as I know more, you will be my first phone call."

"Okay," I muttered.

An awkward silence fell between us before he cleared his throat. "Well, as long as you are okay, I should get back to work."

"Sure. Thank you for checking," I told him.

He floundered in the dead space for a few seconds longer before telling me goodbye. As I set the phone back on its cradle, I sank down to the ground next to it. Even hearing someone's voice had done wonders for the fear that raked through my body. Reyes was on the case, and that gave me comfort. I stood up slowly, letting the dark room penetrate my mind as I tried to get control of it.

I heard the footsteps before the doorknob started to move. The fear that I'd felt when the phone rang was nothing compared to the crippling anxiety that was taking over now. Outside, the intruder tried to get into the locked door. My fingers flew to the phone once again, ready to call back my knight in shining armor at the first sign of trouble. I still couldn't shake the feeling that someone was watching me very closely.

Someone pounded on the door, and my heart thumped.

"Damnit, Annabeth! I forgot my keycard for work. Let me in!" my mother yelled.

I sighed, slipping back against the wall for a second before she pounded on the door again. Jumping to my feet, I ran to the door and quickly jerked it open. She glared at me, shoving past where I was standing and heading for the kitchen.

"Jesus, it's like a mausoleum in here!" she hissed. "Why is everything so dark? Did you go around and close all the blinds?"

She looked back at me and I nodded my head sheepishly. "It was . . . it was just a lot of light."

Rolling her eyes, she snatched her work badge from the counter and stormed past me. "This is getting ridiculous! I wasn't even gone for five minutes and look at you. You look like you've seen a ghost. I'm wondering if I should have taken you out of the hospital at all. Are you sure this is where you want to be?"

She was scolding me like a child. My cheeks flushed red. I felt like a scared little kid and I hated every part of it. I didn't want to be the weak and timid creature waiting to be rescued like the woman in fairy tales. I wanted to make my own destiny. Shooting her a stern gaze back, I nodded my head in defiance.

"This is my home. Of course this is where I want to be. Like I said, it was just a little too bright. I was thinking about taking a nap."

Her knowing eyes traveled up and back down my body. She knew I was lying as much as I knew she wasn't happy about my being there. Even behind the looks of anger and pain that she kept shooting in my direction, I knew that there was care and concern. My mother was never great at expressing her emotions.

"Fine," she muttered as she jerked open the door again. "I guess you should get back to your nap then."

"Have a great day at work," I hissed.

I already had a plan for my afternoon formulating in my head. I wasn't going to sit around and wait for Gregory's kidnapper to make contact with me again. No, I was going to take action and prove to my mother that I was capable of being more than a scared barn mouse. The time for action had come, and I was through letting other people tell me what was best for myself and my son.

"Are you sure you are okay?" she asked softly one last time.

I smiled at her. I could hear the change in her tone. She was worried about both of her children, not just the one in the hospital.

"I really am, Mom," I whispered earnestly.

"Good," she said quickly before jerking open the

door. "I believe you. Have a good day, honey. I hope you can find some answers."

"Thanks, Mom," I whispered. It felt like the first genuine moment we'd had since the whole ordeal had started.

My heart raced when I saw that the front porch wasn't empty. My mother spun around to see who the shadow belonged to. Her glare leveled as her body stiffened.

"Hello, Jacob," she hissed.

CHAPTER SIX

"Hello, Amy," Jacob said, his voice thick with loathing. "How are you doing on this fine afternoon?"

"My son is clinging to his life and my grandson is missing. How do you think I am doing? What do you want? I don't remember needing any work done," she snapped back.

"You know, you didn't always dislike me so much. Remember when we used to get along?"

"We all make bad judgement calls. I asked you a question," Mom hissed.

"Mother!" I hissed at her. "What has gotten into you? Jacob is here as a friend, I'm sure."

"You can have all the friends you want. Doesn't

mean I have to like them," she snapped back at me. "I have to go to work."

She shoved past him, to my surprise. Given how much she disliked Jacob, she didn't often leave the two of us alone. It didn't matter that I was an adult. Her distrust for him ran deep. So, when she didn't try to make him leave along with her, I wasn't sure how to react. Part of me hoped that she'd finally seen that Jacob was big and burly but ultimately harmless. The sinister side of my mind knew that she was simply giving up.

"Mind if I come in?" he asked, looking past me to the living room.

My hand tightened on the door. Jacob had been a guest in our house so many times that I shouldn't have hesitated. His gaze leveled on me, shocked that I wasn't immediately stepping aside. As a blush rose to his scarred cheeks, I knew that I had to make a decision. The longer I left him standing there without a decision either way, the more awkward the whole situation became.

Finally, I had to make a move. "Sure, but I can't talk long. I was just getting ready to go down to the police station."

His eyes widened, an anger cloaked behind his thick veil. "Oh? I thought we'd agreed that I was going to handle them."

My thoughts raced. I hated trying to lie. From across the room, I spotted a picture of Gregory and took a deep breath. "The detective just needs a better picture of Gregory."

I went to the mantle. The Christmas tree next to it should have brought me comfort, but now it stood as a stark reminder of what and who was missing. My heart ached as I looked down at the photo of Tom and Gregory that we'd taken just days before his abduction. They were wearing matching smiles and identical hideous sweatshirts. Each green concoction had floral blubs that lit up when pressed.

"Gregory thought this was the greatest sweatshirt ever," I whispered as my fingers ran over my son's face. "Tom hates them, but he wore it for hours to make Gregory happy."

"It's okay to be okay, Annabeth. Just let me take care of everything, all right?" Jacob said.

His tone was soothing, but I could feel him standing closer to me than before. There were barely two feet between us. I shuddered, a cold chill running down my body and making my stomach churn. I gripped the picture of my son close to my chest. I didn't know if it was the intimacy of the house, the pain in my heart, or the darkness, but suddenly, the overwhelming realization that I was alone with Jacob came flooding back to me.

Stepping away from him, I carefully took the photo from its frame and plastered a smile on my face. "Well, thank you for stopping by, but I really should get going. The detective is expecting me."

It was so strange to be lying to Jacob, but lately, I couldn't trust anyone in my life. He glared down at the photo, snatching it from my hands before I could stop him.

"Why don't you let me take care of this?" he said in a sharp tone. "I told you I would, after all."

I bit my lip, turning away from him. On one hand, it would get him out of the house. I didn't really feel comfortable with him there, but my mother had been so pushy earlier that I'd let my emotions get the best of me. I'd welcomed him into my home to spite her. She and I both knew that what I really needed was to be alone. It was just too quiet to be there on my own. Everything made me jump out of my skin.

"Sure," I muttered. "You know what? That would be really helpful."

Without waiting for him to respond, I grabbed his arm and led him back to the front door. He seemed to relish the touch of my hand, even as I was shoving him out the door. Spinning back around to face me, he grabbed ahold of my hand and gently squeezed it. I clenched my jaw together and tried not to rip myself free from him.

"You don't want me to stay and visit for a while? Your mother is at work now. Do you really think being alone is what's best?"

"I'm fine," I shot back at him. "You said you wanted to help, and this is what is going to help the most."

"Annabeth," he said. "I'm worried about you. It's so dark in there. Should I be calling your head doctor again?"

I rolled my eyes. "She is my therapist, and no, Jacob. I am going to be fine. I just want to be alone and try to piece together what happened ten years ago. The more I can give the police, the better chance they have of catching this guy and bringing home my son."

"We will find him," he promised reassuringly.

"I know. Thanks for running that down for me too," I said as I started to close the door.

"Do you want me to stop back by when I'm done? I can grab us some lunch if you want."

I shook my head vigorously. Standing there with the door open was making my panic rise even more. The killer could be watching us, waiting to find a way to get back into my home. I slowly shut the door, even as Jacob was trying to find a reason to come back. With one final shake of my head, the door was closed and I was alone again. The alarm signaled, letting me know that no one was getting into the house without my permission.

"Come on, girl," I told myself. "You've got to figure this out. You know that monster better than anyone else."

I pulled myself away from the door and grabbed the wireless phone, tucking it into my back pocket as I jogged up the steps. When I reached Gregory's room, my heart sank to my stomach. Everything looked just the same as he'd left it days before. It was neat and orderly, just like him. Nothing seemed out of place. I ran my fingers along his spotless desk, taking in the row of neatly lined up pencils.

Unable to bear waiting for information, I called the private number Reyes had given me. When he didn't answer, my mind started to race.

"Maybe he's just busy," I told myself. "He has other cases besides Gregory's."

At once, my mind started to play tricks on me, wondering if the police were going to be any help at all and questioning whether I was even worthy of having a son. I shook my head, trying desperately to get the morbidly depressing thoughts out of my mind. I couldn't call anyone else and tell them what was going on. They would just tell me to take my anti-depressants, but I knew that I couldn't. They had a habit of blocking out my ability to remember what had happened so long ago.

I needed those memories to help me find Gregory, even if the police were too busy. Making my way back into my own bedroom, I set the phone down on the table and slumped back against the neatly made bed. My mother's work, I was sure. She liked to clean when she had a lot on her mind. I missed the chaos that always seemed to work for me. Closing my eyes, I forced the dark images of the present out of my mind and started shuffling backward.

They'd never found the location I was being held at, even though they searched the area several times. Disoriented and in shock, I'd run for miles through the woods for days before I found help. The secluded cabin had looked like hundreds of others scattered throughout the wilderness. Several of them had been in families for generations, never plotted out or even on maps. My fingers ran down my arms, feeling the bumps from where thorns had ripped at my skin.

No one was chasing me then. My captor had passed out for the night after forcing himself on me. I'd only escaped because of pure dumb luck. Otherwise, I would have died in that awful place. Whoever he was, he couldn't hold his liquor. After a few drinks, I heard the creaking on his bed above me, his body slumping down for the night while I was left in the darkness. He'd drunk too much, actually. The slip cost him his prisoner as I fumbled with the steps and finally broke my way free into the bitter night.

From the nightstand, the phone started to ring, and I jumped. I held it in my hands for a few seconds, weighing the decision to answer it. The killer never called during the day, but maybe he was changing the game. Maybe I could trade him my own life for my son's.

"Hello?" I answered in a raspy voice.

"Annabeth?" Gabriel said quickly.

I let out a sigh of relief. "Detective, thank you for calling me back."

"You called?" he said, obviously confused. "Sorry. I was running down a few leads. I was wondering if you could come down to the station?"

"What?" I gasped. "Have you found Gregory?"

"No," he blurted out quickly. "But we have a suspect. I'd like you to come down and see if you can identify him."

"Yes!" I said, my voice practically a scream. "Absolutely. I will be there in a few minutes."

"Okay," Reyes said carefully. "Don't get your hopes up though. He does meet all the criteria we're looking for, but still, it's a long shot."

"Yeah, sure," I said as I jogged down the steps. Without thinking, I burst out the front door, not even bothering to end the call with Detective Reyes before dropping the phone near the door and dashing to my car.

"I'm coming for you, Gregory," I whispered into the wind. "I'm coming for you, baby."

CHAPTER SEVEN

I hated driving. I always had. Even as a teen, my mother had to force me at eighteen to get my license. There was too much chaos in the world for me to feel safe behind the wheel. Granted, in the years since Greg's passing, I'd had little choice but to learn to control that fear of other drivers. It had become an issue of keeping Gregory safe, and for that reason, I suffered through the traffic. Now, it was more important than ever that I keep my mind on the road.

What I couldn't understand was road rage. How could people get so angry over something so small? The thoughts that were going through my mind were anything but pleasant. Who was the man they thought took my baby? Was he okay? Would the kidnapper tell us where he was, or had he already done something terrible to my baby? The fear inside me was replaced with a blinding rage at whomever they'd caught. I wasn't sure if I wanted to find out the truth or if it was best if I never knew.

As I pulled onto the outer belt that connected most of the city, I noticed a brown van following a few cars behind me. It wasn't anything significant, but something about it still caught my eye.

"Come on, Annabeth, get your shit together," I muttered as I got off on the exit for the police station.

I watched the van, now three cars behind me as it, too, pulled off the exit. My heart was beating so loudly I could hear it in my ears. For a second, I thought about calling Reyes on my cellphone, but the overly cautious voice inside my head wouldn't let me do anything but keep two hands firmly planted on the wheel of my car. That was how people ended up dead, when they got distracted while driving. Plus, the exit took me into downtown. Lots of cars headed that way.

The lunchtime rush of traffic slowed my drive down to a crawl. As the police station came into view, I made a decision. Without slowing down anymore, I drove past the station and turned down the road next to it. It wasn't used as often, a few cars scattered on the side of the road as the patrons of local bars drank away their problems. If only I could do the same thing. Getting sloshed wouldn't bring my baby back though.

"You are being ridiculous," I whispered.

Just as I reached the end of the road, I glanced back in my mirror and saw the van turn into the narrow street as well. The brown van was following me. I was now confidant of that. I fumbled with the phone in the passenger seat as it crept closer to where I was parked. Who was I going to call though? The second I pulled up to the police station, they would probably keep going. Or worse, I could be losing my mind entirely and the van could be some poor florist just trying to make his rounds for the day.

They were almost on my bumper now, and part of me wanted to wait and see if I would recognize the driver. On the other hand, though, Reyes said they had a suspect in custody, so what the hell was I doing being paranoid about a van? I gunned the engine, peeling out onto the street amidst the traffic and making a wide circle of the police station. The van stayed close on my tail and I knew that they were following me.

As the police station came back into view, I had to make a decision. I hated making decisions on the spot. Greg always told me if our house was burning down, I'd be stuck in the flames, wondering what pair of shoes to wear to save my life. Just thinking about him warmed my heart and gave me a little boost of courage. Jerking the wheel to the right, I pulled suddenly into a parking place right in front of the police station.

The van skidded to a stop a few feet away, still too far for me to get a good look at the driver. I thought about jumping out but before I could make a decision, it sped away, the sound of screeching tires burning into my brain. Even after the van was gone, my heart wouldn't slow back down. I let my hands drop off the wheel as they shook violently. Everything was shaking, even my toes, as fear crippled me.

I couldn't see the van anymore. It had disappeared, but I didn't feel any safer. The police entrance was twenty feet away, yet I couldn't seem to get my legs to work. Even my hands were refusing to cooperate as I tried to reach for the door handle. I closed my eyes, taking a few deep breaths like Dr. Andrews had taught me to do when I felt a panic attack coming on. I was finishing the last of ten breaths when my phone started to ring.

With a dry mouth, I jumped and answered it, my fingers finally cooperating. "Hello?"

"Hey, I stopped back by your place and you weren't there. Is everything okay?" Jacob asked.

I sighed, frustration starting to creep in. How could they find my son and get ahold of me if Jacob wouldn't give me even an hour's time alone? I knew he was worried—we all were!

"I'm fine, I just needed to get out of the house." The lie slipped out before I could stop myself.

"Oh? Just taking a cruise? You know I would have gone with you. I know how much you hate to drive."

"It's fine," I muttered. "I had a few errands to run anyway."

"Anything I can help with?"

"No," I whispered. "I'm actually at the police station. They think they might have a suspect. I wanted to get down here as fast as possible."

"A suspect?" he pressed. "I thought we agreed that I was going to deal with all that."

"Well, Jacob, you weren't the one captured and tortured for weeks, so maybe they need me there to help them with the matter," I snapped.

"Jesus, Annabeth," he seethed. "I was just trying to help. If you want to be left alone then just say so. God, I thought Gregory was more important that our own feelings."

I closed my eyes, the aching hurt of my missing son creeping back in. It was so wrong of me to snap at Jacob when he was only trying to be a friend.

"I'm sorry, Jacob," I whispered.

"Don't bother. I didn't get a chance to drop off the picture of Gregory at the station. I can bring it by now, though, and we can go talk with those pigs together."

"No," I said firmly. "I need to do this alone."

"You can barely stay in your house alone, but you want to get questioned by a bunch of cops solo? You really don't know how to accept help when you need it, Annabeth. Does your mother know that you are there?"

"My mother has nothing to do with this. She's working, and I don't want to get her hopes up if this suspect doesn't work out."

"Well, what do you know about him, huh? What makes them think that this is the guy who took my boy?"

"*Your* boy?" I shot back. "Jacob—"

"Oh, stop it!" he interrupted. "You know what I mean. I love him like he's my own and you are acting like a crazy woman, trying to keep me out of the loop!"

"I am doing no such thing."

His words rang true, though I wouldn't admit it. I did want to keep him out of all of this. I didn't like the way that he and Reyes spoke to each other. I could see myself getting along rather well with the detective, but not with Jacob there, being overprotective. He meant well. He just didn't know how to express it at times. I felt guilty for the way I'd been treating my friend. After all, he was practically family.

"I'm sorry, Jacob," I told him. "It's just been a rough few days. I promise to let you know if they find out anything about Gregory."

"I still don't like it. You told me I was in charge of

the police, and now you are sneaking around behind my back to go talk to them."

"It's their job," I reminded him. "They are the ones looking for Gregory. I wish you would stop trying to make me feel guilty and accept that I need to work with them. You have a business to run."

"Family is more important than business. What do you know about the suspect they brought in?"

"Not much."

A dark van pulled onto the road and my heart started to race again. It slowly went past, and I saw a mother yelling at children in the backseat. Letting out a heavy sigh, I closed my eyes and tried to get my heartrate back down.

"Annabeth, what's going on?" Jacob asked.

I knew he would find out somehow. "There was someone following me earlier. They're gone now, but I'm sure of it."

A long pause followed my confession before he snapped. "That's it, I'm coming down there. You aren't safe alone, obviously."

"Jacob, no," I said quickly.

"It's not up for discussion! Someone is following you and they have one suspect. How much worse does this need to get before you realize that you can't handle it on your own?"

"I'm not alone," I reminded him. "I have Detective Reyes and my mother and—"

"Oh, Jesus, why don't you just fuck him and get it out of the way, so we can all get back to trying to find your son! God, you would think that you'd have your priorities in order!"

"Jacob!" I blurted out. My cheeks flushed red. "How dare—"

"No, I'm done with it," he said quickly. "I'm coming down there."

I wanted to yell at him to keep away from the whole situation, but I already felt terrible for yelling at him before. The last thing I needed was for him to show up and make the whole process even more difficult. Something had to keep him happy while I took care of things.

"Please, Jacob, I can do this on my own, but I promise I will give you a call when I'm done, and maybe we can grab a late lunch."

"Really?" he asked, his tone obviously lighter.

"Really," I muttered in reply.

He'd wanted to go on a lunch date for years, but I always shot him down. Now, it seemed like the only thing I could do to keep him happy. It was like juggling multiple people at once. Sometimes, Jacob could be the best friend a girl could ask for. Other times, though, he didn't know when to stop pressing. He knew just what buttons to push to get me to cave. I hated it. Still, he was family. What was I supposed to do?

"Yeah. I will give you a call, okay?"

"I still don't like your going in there on your own. Those police officers can be manipulative."

"Reyes is a good detective. We need to have a little faith in him if we want him to find Gregory," I reminded Jacob.

"Right," he grumbled.

"Please stop reading so much into this, okay? I need to go now. He's waiting for me."

"Well, so am I, so make it quick, okay? I have a company to run. I can't be waiting around all day for you to finish up."

"I will go as fast as I can," I told him, guilt washing over me as I thought about how much my friend needed me.

"Fine," he snapped before hanging up.

I winced at his abrupt end to the call. He would get over it. He always did. I looked around the parking lot one last time to make sure there were no vans. Then, taking a deep breath, I jumped out of my car and briskly walked up the steps to the police headquarters. The glass door opened and a smiling young woman in uniform behind the counter asked if I needed help. Even as I was explaining who I was, Reyes rounded the corner.

Our eyes locked and the cold barriers of my heart started to melt away. There was something about him, something so honest and pure, that I was reminded of Gregory. He smiled at me, walking out into the lobby and softly brushing a hand against my arm. My stomach did a little flip, tingling with excitement. All the problems with Jacob, the van that seemed to be following me, they all washed away with his touch.

"It's good to see you," he said softly. "Are you ready for this?"

I nodded, unsure.

"I will be with you the entire time, okay?"

"Do you promise?"

He grinned, sending my heart fluttering once again. "I promise. You aren't ever going to be alone while you're here. We will nail this son of a bitch, okay?"

"Okay," I whispered. For the first time, I said something that I hadn't said in years. "I trust you."

CHAPTER EIGHT

His expression changed in an instant when he saw how distraught I was. Quickly pulling me over to a row of empty chairs, Gabriel sat down next to me. I was still shaking from the whole ordeal, and the conversation with Jacob hadn't helped any either. Struggling with my emotions, I tried to get myself under control.

"What's going on? You look like you've seen a ghost. Did the kidnapper contact you?" he asked quickly.

I shook my head. "No, but someone was following me."

"Are you sure?"

I nodded. "I'm sure. I drove around the block and he kept following me."

"Did you get a license plate or a look at the guy?"

"No, I didn't even think about it. I thought you had the guy in custody!" I said a little more aggressively than intended.

"No, I'm sorry, but we can't arrest someone just because of similarities. I wanted you to come down and look at a couple pictures though. If anything looks familiar, we can bring him in for questioning."

"Can't you just go look through his house?"

"Well," he muttered. "We can, but I don't think it would do us any good. You said you were held in the mountains, but this guy lives in an apartment downtown. He is a registered sex offender, which is why his name popped up on our radar. Some things about his case and yours seem a lot alike."

"I don't understand," I told him. "Do you know what kind of car he drives? Is it a brown van, by chance?"

Gabriel flipped through a small notebook he'd brought with him. "No, sorry. But that doesn't mean he isn't our guy. Creeps like him find ways around our system. He could buy a vehicle with cash and never put legitimate tags on them. I just don't want to rule him out because someone followed you. Plus—"

"Then let's get this started. I need to find my son," I interjected.

"Good, we can start right away, but there is something else you need to know," he said, seemingly nervous. "A news station picked up your story. We think someone at the hospital leaked it. Normally, we would put a ban on the case, but with kidnappings, it can help to have the public on the lookout for him."

"Oh," I muttered. "Okay."

My mother wasn't going to be happy that Gregory's kidnapping was all over the news. She liked to keep things quiet. I didn't really care about her feelings on the subject anymore. Part of me had to shut down and let go of her and Jacob's feelings about the situation. Greg had always trusted me to do what was right. I wasn't going to fail him now. The memory of my late husband made my eyes prickle with tears.

"Are you okay?" whispered Reyes. "Maybe we should wait another day to do all of this. I don't want to give you more than you can handle."

"And what about Gregory? How many days does he have to handle the situation while I sit on my hands? No, we are going to push forward. You said you had some pictures for me to see?"

He nodded but didn't move. "You know, when I lost the girls' mother, I never thought I was going to get over it."

"This isn't about me," I snapped. "And I am not going to lose Gregory, okay?"

"No, no, I understand that. I just want to make

sure that you're taking care of yourself during this time. You won't be any use to anyone if you're too weak or distraught to take care of him when we get him back."

"You mean 'if' we get him back? I've watched crime shows before, you know. I'm not an idiot."

"I know you aren't an idiot," he stammered in shock. "I would never imply that. But these photos are of a crime scene. This guy was no joke. If it gets to be too much, you just need to let me know, okay?"

"Sure," I muttered, still unsure. "What's his name?"

"His name is Morrie Jenkins. He's well into his sixties by now, but his crime took place in the late eighties."

"That's awful old to be stalking someone. Why do you think he's connected?" I asked.

Gabriel shifted in his seat. "There are a couple of things this guy has going for us. He was released the year before the attack on you and your husband took place. Plus, at the time, he was an avid hunter."

"I'm sure there were lots of people let out of jail that year. Please tell me you have something more concrete."

He grinned. "I do, I'm just trying to take things slow, okay?"

"Okay," I whispered. He really was a good man. "What's his story?"

Gabriel looked around the lobby as a pair in uniform strolled in and greeted him. "Why don't we go back to my office?"

My face paled, flashes of him cuffing me and raping me filling my mind. I covered my hands, trying to stop the trembling. At the hospital, it was one thing. But being left alone with a man behind closed doors was another. Even if he did make me feel comfortable in the time we'd spent together, I wasn't ready to be alone with him just yet. Especially not when he was in his own element.

He saw the change in my demeanor and changed course at once. "Or, we have a conference room we could use. We can close the door, but it's got glass walls, so everyone can see what's going on. I just thought you'd feel more comfortable away from the hustle and bustle."

"Thank you," I said quietly. "The conference room sounds perfect."

He got up and led me through a secured door and back into the heart of the precinct. People milled around, but no one seemed to pay any attention to us. There was an old woman sitting in a chair and talking with a set of officers. Another man, younger and covered in grime, was handcuffed on a bench. Everything about the place seemed so normal, just like I'd seen on television. When he led me into the conference room, I felt a little surer of my decision to be there.

Reyes hadn't been lying. Glass walls kept everything perfectly in view of the rest of the police officers. I stepped in and sat down on the far side of the long table as Gabriel spoke to a younger looking officer before the man darted away. He quickly reappeared with a stack of manila folders. Reyes poked his head in before the younger officer left.

"Do you want coffee or anything?" he asked.

My phone vibrated. It was Jacob. An unusual burst of aggravation coursed through me. "No, I just want to get this over with."

"Sure," he muttered.

Taking a seat next to me, he pulled out a piece of paper and started writing. "Okay, I'm going to have you fill out this form so I can forward it to my team in car retrieval. This should get us the information on the van."

"Okay," I whispered.

I started writing down everything that had happened that afternoon. It seemed almost mundane compared to everything else going on in my small world. I wrote quickly, trying to keep my handwriting legible while still moving at a fast pace. When I was finished, I shoved the paper in Gabriel's direction.

"Now tell me about this man, Morrie," I demanded.

He sighed, pulling a file from the stack and flipping it open. The police report was attached to an inmate's photo. Jenkins looked older than what Reyes told me, but I had to assume prison life wasn't easy.

"In the eighties, the officers got a tip after this idiot was caught too close to a park. He was a registered offender even back then. That's the only reason we linked him to the attack and found the little boy."

"A pedophile?" My voice was hoarse. "You think he wants to abuse Gregory?"

"It's a very real possibility, I'm afraid." He shifted in his seat. "I don't know how much detail I should go into with this. I don't want to make things harder."

Glaring at him, I snatched the file from his hands. "I want you to tell me everything. Just like I told you, okay? Start from the beginning."

Gabriel looked shocked at my force but nodded his head. "Okay. But you'll tell me if you need a break?"

"Sure," I curtly replied.

"In nineteen eighty-seven, Janice and Micha Goldstein were at their home in Pennybrook."

"I know that area. It's nice," I interjected.

"Very. Even back then, it was an up and coming neighborhood. The Goldsteins were just about to sit down for dinner when Jenkins broke into their home.

He entered through the front door and took down Janice first. He used a taser on her. When Micha, whom we don't believe he knew was home, came into the room, he used a baseball bat and clubbed him over the head. Patrick was nine at the time."

"Oh, my God," I whispered.

"He took Patrick and held him prisoner for a year before the police found his hideout. In that time, he sexually assaulted the boy up to five times a day."

"That . . ." I swallowed. "That sounds like what the man did to me."

"Oh, shit," Reyes said before quickly recovering. "I'm sorry, I didn't mean—"

I lifted my hand, stopping him mid-sentence. "This is what you need to know. I understand that. It's fine. My captor would come five, six, seven times a day. It was always something new, something twisted."

"Well, we found Patrick and we will find Gregory. Now, we have some photos here from the crime scene. It would help us if you could look at them and try to connect it to where you were being held. If we can, then we can arrest Morrie and start the process from there. Hopefully, he can lead us to Gregory."

"You really think this is the guy?" I asked, running my fingers over the photo.

"Do you?"

"I don't know. I can't be sure. It was so dark, and

I've blocked out so much of it. He doesn't seem large enough though."

"That would make sense. This is an old photo. I have CPS finding me a more recent one, but he's put on almost a hundred pounds since the eighties. To be honest, he'd mostly fallen off our radar. The man's been in therapy and on meds for most of his life outside of jail. We haven't even had a report of him being near a school or park since his release."

"So, what makes you think he's connected?"

"Something in the boy's statement," he said as he flipped through another file. "Here it is."

I looked down at the report, reading the typed letter and desperately trying to keep myself from breaking down into tears at his account.

'The rooms were dark, like a maze that I couldn't figure out. My belly always felt funny while I was there, but it was okay. When he gave me the happy juice, the pain stopped for a while. It always came back, though, whenever 'Daddy' came to play doctor with me. I told him that it hurts but he doesn't listen. He told me I was a bad boy, and this is what happens to bad boys. I promised him I wouldn't cry anymore, but it

hurts, everything hurts. My arms, my legs, all over.'

I sucked in a sharp breath, trying to keep the sobs at bay. Quickly turning the paper over, I closed my eyes. I couldn't read any more of it. Every time I started to, I saw what was happening through the young boy's eyes. I thought about my own son and the suffering he could be enduring.

"Hey," Reyes said softly, his hand sliding over mine.

I jerked it away. "I can't, I'm sorry. I don't want to read anymore. You said you had pictures that I had to see."

He nodded slowly. "Are you sure about this? You look a little green around the edges."

"I will be fine. If it will help us, then I will get through it."

"Okay," Gabriel said, still looking doubtful. He pulled out another folder and slid it over to me without opening it. "I have to warn you, though, that these are pictures of his house, the basement where he was holding Patrick, and where we found his parents."

The file felt heavy in my hands, like it was weighed down with the shame and horror of what had occurred.

Reyes cleared his throat and I looked up at his kind, dark eyes.

"I'm going to give you a little space to look these over, but I'll be back in a few minutes, okay? Please, Annabeth, if it becomes too much, just take a break, okay? We can always bring in Patrick to take a look again."

"And make that poor man relive everything that's happened to him?" I questioned. "Absolutely not. As a survivor, I can tell you that this would fuck up anyone's world, having to go through it all a second time. Leave the poor man alone. Let his past stay in the past."

Reyes stood just as a female officer came to the door. "We've got a few reporters out here who want to talk to Ms. Simmons. What should I tell them?"

"Tell them she is not, and will not ever be, making a statement," he snapped.

My heart fluttered at his authority. He looked down at me and smiled. "Actually, I will go deal with them. Officer Gander, can you stay close in case Ann—" Reyes blushed. Ms. Simmons needs anything?"

"Sure, Detective," the woman said, smiling at me. "I'll be right out here at this desk if you need me."

"Thanks," I muttered.

"I'll be right back. I'm going to go deal with those sharks. If anything looks familiar in the photos, just set it aside and we can go over it when I get back, okay?"

"Okay," I promised him.

I watched him go, my eyes lingering a little longer than they should have on his rear. The desire that was stirring inside me quickly dampened as I looked down at the folder. No one else could help my son except me. I was the only one who knew where he was being held. As my phone rang a second time, I took a deep breath. Reaching down, I shut it off. Anything, anyone else, they could all wait. I knew that going through the images was going to take all the strength that I had.

CHAPTER NINE

My hand moved slowly to open the folder. The first image wasn't as bad as I expected. It was an outdated photo of a seemingly normal living room. The only indication that it was a police report was a stack of yellow numbers in the corner. Three had been removed, their bold, black numbers sitting on the carpet in the picture. One of them was next to a broken glass of some sort. The others were next to dark stains on the carpet.

I didn't need to be a detective to know that they were bloodstains. Given the circumstances, it was an easier photo for me to start with. Carefully, as if it could break, I slid it to the other side of the opened folder and looked at the second one. The stark difference in images came as a shock to me. I sucked in a sharp breath and looked away. They hadn't done a very good job of documenting the Goldsteins' home, but Jenkins's place was well photographed.

"Come on," I whispered to myself. "Do it for Gregory."

Dragging my gaze back to the images in front of me, I had to gather all of my strength. It was a house in the city, perfectly normal looking, if not a little rundown. Nothing about it said there was a pedophile living inside. Everything was just what you would expect in a slightly poor area of town for that timeframe. A bland, off-white house sat pinched between two others with run-down wire fencing wrapping around an unkempt lawn.

The next image made me more curious than upset. Inside the home looked just as ideal as the outside. The faded photo showed a living room and part of a bathroom. The threadbare couch sat near a dinner tray and an old, large box television. The faded carpeting had seen better days, and there were no photos on the walls or decorations to speak of. Everything about the photo seemed almost sloppy. I flipped to the next image and my heart pounded a little harder.

It was an image of a bookcase, just slightly ajar, and behind it, a dark staircase. I knew that I was getting close to the pictures that would really upset me. My fingers lingered over the photo, wondering if I should keep going or let someone else compare photos. But there was nothing else for them to compare it to. I was the other photo. My memories were what they needed. Taking a calming breath, I flipped the page and shuddered.

Even though I tried to close my eyes against the image, it was already too late. The shot flashed through my brain. It was a simple room with a bed in the corner. Near the foot of the bed was what made my heart break. A chain, obviously used and dirty, was sitting on the floor. It was too small to hold an adult but just the right size for a child. The same matching chains were also at the head of the bed.

I shook my head, begging for it not to be true. My son couldn't be this monster's new pet. What if he had escalated? What if Jenkins knew that the police were onto him and decided to kill my baby? I felt a panic attack as it started to creep in. I shoved the chair away from the table and closed my eyes. I'd had more panic attacks in the last hour than I'd had in months. I started to question everything I was doing.

What could I have done differently to keep my baby safe? The police had every harassing phone call on record, but it wasn't enough. It would never be enough if I didn't get him back. More than anything, I wanted to hunt down Jenkins and put him six feet under where he belonged. The hair on my neck stood up. I felt someone watching me. I quickly scanned the area and saw the culprit. The officer from before was sitting at her desk, watching me. She looked ready to run into the room at a moment's notice.

"Of course she is," I muttered under my breath. "Everyone here thinks I'm a nut job."

Realizing that they all probably thought I was insane gave me a boost of energy to keep going. I had to prove them wrong. If anyone was going to crack the case, it would be the only eyewitness that they had, and that was me. Grinding my teeth together, I looked away from the woman and scooted back up to the table, taking in the images once again.

The next photo was not easy for me to cope with. Patrick had been right. The basement Morrie was keeping him in was a maze. Rough-cut lumber built up and sectioned off smaller areas of the basement into bedrooms. When I saw the second bed in its own room, my heart sank. Jenkins wasn't just a pedophile. He liked his numbers. I flipped through another two images, both of them the same with just minor differences.

"Four," I whispered.

"How are you doing?" said a familiar voice.

I jumped as I looked up, nearly falling out of my chair. "Jesus, Reyes, you scared me."

His eyes grew wide. "I'm sorry. I didn't mean to."

"It's okay. It's going fine," I said. I had to ask. I had to know for my own sanity. "How many?"

He didn't need me to elaborate. "Ten, as far as we know. There were ten people who came forward. A few of the missing children, though, we think were his victims too, but we couldn't charge him."

"Any you let that bastard back out on the street?"

He cringed. "It's not really my call. Once someone does their time, we can't keep holding them."

"And now this prick is out there doing the same thing to my son, and you guys won't make a move against him. Wow." I whistled.

"Annabeth," he cautioned. "I've been at this for a long time. I know that you want us to go in there, guns blazing, but what if we are wrong? Or what if we are right and we don't follow protocol? He will be out on the streets again because of a technicality."

"Fine," I snapped. "Whatever. I'll let you know when I'm done going through the pictures."

"Are you sure you don't want me in here with you?" he asked

"I'm positive. I don't want to be around anyone right now. Just give me a few more minutes."

"Okay, one more thing. Your friend, Jacob, called the station looking for you. I told him I couldn't give out any personal information, including your whereabouts, and he got pretty pissed. Should we be looking into him?"

I rolled my eyes. "No. He's harmless, just a little overprotective."

"A little?"

I chuckled. "Okay, a lot, but he's fine. If he calls again, just tell him I'm busy, okay? Thanks."

I turned back to the photos in front of me, ending the conversation. I didn't look up when the door softly shut behind him. My playful thoughts from before were burnt off as soon as I started digging. As I turned the next photo over, my heart sank. It was a photo of the entire basement's blueprints. The officer who made them left size and other indications of the basement in the corners.

They'd been thorough, even back in the eighties. They tracked everything, from where he got the lumber to the plumber he'd called to put in a makeshift shower. I had to wonder what the man thought when he went down there. Did he even think that something strange was going on? Would the man still be alive to question?

Everything about the layout felt outdated and half-assed, like he hadn't put that much thought into what he was doing. And why would he? He was after little kids, not an architecture award. I had to find out if he was the same man. Taking a deep breath, I closed my eyes and let the memories flood back again. I saw Greg, lying in a pool of his own blood. The hands on my face restricted my breathing.

And the smell, it was overpoweringly sweet and bitter at the same time. Like his cleaning lady had tried to cover the stench of something dark. He knew better though. The more time I spent as his sexual prisoner, my rapist and his habits became clearer. The man would always clean my jail himself, taking care that I never saw his face. Or perhaps, I did see it, but my mind had destroyed that image long ago. It was the only way for me to protect myself against the nightmares.

They needed a face. Or some other detail that could point them in the direction of my husband's killer. I searched back through the memories, doing my best to use blinders against the pain and torture he was submitting me to. Beyond the searing wounds, past the stench of his body, and above the feel of woodchips under my skin, I felt something wet.

Bile rose to the back of my throat as I realized it was his sweat dropping down onto my face. I shook my body, my face trying to get rid of it. I thought that I was lost in the memory. I would never escape it now. But someone grabbed me by the arms, shaking me and calling my name. I followed the voice back into the police station. Gabriel was watching me, his eyes full of fear.

"Annabeth!" he yelled.

I gasped, grabbing his hands and nodding my head. "I'm fine, I'm sorry. I shouldn't have done that."

"Done what? Are you okay? You've got to stop doing that to me. God, should I have a doctor here?"

I cringed at his cold tone. How could I be surprised though? I knew how high-maintenance I was. My mother constantly reminded me of that fact when I woke her at night screaming in fear. My shoulders stiffened. I was determined to see this through to the end, without needing someone like the detective to lean on.

Clearing my throat, I dropped my shaking hands into my lap and out of his sight. "Sorry. I'm fine, really. What can you tell me about this place again? It looks like he was in a rush."

Reyes shrugged. "I don't think he had much time to assemble it, to be honest. He was on the run when we caught up to him."

I shook my head. "No. The place that I was being held at was well-constructed. He cared about it."

"If this was a temporary place, though," Reyes mused.

"I just don't know. I can't see him ever leaving that place. It was designed to be a maze. It must have taken him years."

"But crimes like these can escalate. It's possible he was forced to move after you got loose. He couldn't know that you would have amnesia. Maybe he just panicked."

"I don't know. I guess. I might never know without meeting him again."

Reyes shifted uneasily. "It would seem my men were able to bring him in for questioning."

My heart started to race. "He is here? Right now?"

Reyes nodded, "He's in the interrogation room right now. I wanted to check in on you first though."

"Can I watch it?" I blurted out. "I mean, can I see you talk to him? I don't know, it might trigger something in my memory."

"Do you really want to risk doing that again?"

"It's not like I have a choice. What would you do if someone kidnapped one of your daughters?" I said quickly.

I saw him wince, though he quickly recovered. "I can let you watch from the room next door, but there is no way in hell you are going anywhere near him, understand?"

I nodded my head vigorously, "Yes, of course. Thank you for allowing me that much."

"Listen," he whispered softly. "We are breaking a lot of rules and regulations here. Can you keep this between us?"

I chuckled. "You don't want me telling Jacob?"

"I know that you trust him, but we still have a job to do. Until I've had a chance to clear him myself, I need to know that you will keep this investigation between us."

"I will," I told him. I knew that there had to be trust between us if we were going to find Gregory.

CHAPTER TEN

I had to admire the stark difference between the Gabriel that I was getting to know and the detective who walked into the interrogation room. I was alone in the next room, watching from a computer monitor while the female officer ran a recording device next to me. Even flying under the radar, they made sure to keep a record of everything.

The two men on screen weren't doing much. It turned out that there was just a lot of paperwork when it came to locking up the bad guys. I wanted to know a little bit more about Gabriel, though, so I welcomed the brief reprieve.

"Detective Reyes is very good at his job," I observed.

The officer chuckled. "He is. If anyone is going to find out what this guy knows, it will be Reyes."

"Does he do this a lot?"

"Not really. This case got to him though."

"Because of his daughters?" I offered.

She nodded. "I wasn't sure what all you knew."

"He shared enough to ease my mind," I told her. "I just want to find my son."

"I can't imagine what you are going through, but I know that not many women would be this brave."

"What do you mean? I feel like I can't do anything right. It seems like I'm a burden on the case."

"Not at all. Having someone here who can give us firsthand accounts isn't something we normally get. The information you have is crucial to finding Gregory." The men on the screen started to talk and we both turned to it. "They are starting."

I watched as Reyes started to question Jenkins. At once, I was consumed with what was happening. Reyes was so calm and collected.

"Mr. Jenkins, do you mind if I call you Morrie?"

The obese man, balding and covered in liver spots, glared at him. "I don't care what you call me. Doesn't change a thing."

"Listen," Reyes said soothingly. "We just want to ask you a few questions. We've been looking over your old case file."

"Now you listen to me, boy. I served my time and I haven't broken the law."

"No one here is saying that you have, Morrie. We just have a couple of questions for you, okay? Calm down."

"What do you want?"

"Where were you two nights ago?"

Morrie scoffed. "Same place as always. In my apartment with this damn bracelet on my ankle."

"That's what happens when you beat people and take their children, Morrie. Society doesn't forget about you until long after you are dead."

"You can track it, okay? Just ask them to tell you exactly where I was. Or what, you think I'm some kind of evil mastermind who can slip out of it?" Morrie coughed as he laughed. "I can't even tie my own shoes anymore, boy. That's what the system does to men like me."

"Pedophiles," hissed Reyes.

"Oh," Morrie snapped, pretending to be intimidated. "Been called a lot worse than that in my day. So, what do you want? Or am I free to go back to my million-dollar lair?"

"A boy was taken," Reyes whispered. "The case is starting to look more and more like your old handiwork there, Morrie."

Gabriel slid out a stack of photos. It took me a

minute to recognize my own home. My brother's blood still stained the carpet in the front hallway. I shuddered but kept my eyes locked on Morrie. His eyes glistened, his crackled lips becoming moist as he looked at images of my son and my home. The bile rose in my throat as I realized what must be going through his mind. I felt a rage like I'd never experienced when I looked at the disgusting man.

"I want to go in there," I hissed.

"Not a chance in hell. Just let Reyes handle this. If he knows anything, he'll crack."

"Look at how he's looking at my son though. I don't like this. I'm never going to know if that's him if you people won't let me face him. What's it going to take to get into that room?"

The officer raised her eyebrow and slowly stood. "It would take an act of God, and unless you sit down, Ms. Simmons, you aren't even going to be in here to watch what Reyes does. Do you understand me?"

I glared at her but slowly sank back down into my seat. You'd think after years of dealing with my mother, I would be accustomed to bossy women. Still, I didn't like backing down to someone I didn't know, someone who clearly had more authority than I did in the disappearance of my own son. I went back to watching the screen, silently and begrudgingly.

"These are from an attack two days ago. One man is in the hospital and we have a little boy missing."

"Oh?" Morrie said, almost amused. "It's all starting to come together now. And you think that I had something to do with all of this?" He chuckled. "Haven't you heard? I'm reformed."

"I saw the way you looked at those pictures. Reformed, my ass. How did you do it, Morrie? Where is the boy?"

"If I knew that, do you think you would have found me in that shitty apartment?"

"It would make a good cover for wherever your real operation is."

"Right, and now we are back to my skills of evading the ankle bracelet."

"You made a lot of enemies in prison. I'm inclined to believe you made a few new friends and learned some skills while you were at it. You play the old fool well, but I know your type. You never stop looking for your next victim. How did you find Gregory? Was it at the park you liked to watch?"

Jenkins's head snapped up. "How do you know about that?"

"We are the police! We know everything," Reyes said as he lost his temper. "I want to know where Gregory is, or else."

"I told you," Morrie seethed. "I don't know

anything about that boy, and if I did, I sure as hell wouldn't help you bastards find him."

"I can have you arrested for obstruction of justice."

"Arrest me for whatever you want, then you'll never find out anything. How do you like that? Huh?"

"Then you do know something?" Reyes whispered.

Morrie glared. "I know enough to keep my mouth shut. I'm not saying another word about it without my lawyer."

Reyes slammed his fist down on the table, making me jump as I watched the screen. "I have a missing kid and you want to talk about lawyers?" He scoffed. "I told them you wouldn't give two shits."

My heart started to race once again as Gabriel headed for the door. This couldn't be it. It couldn't be over already. Not when we were no closer to finding my son than we'd been before. I quickly glanced at my companion, who was deep in thought as she worked with the machine in front of her. My hand twitched as I darted for the door. I jerked it open, making a beeline for the interrogation room before she could stop me.

By pure luck, Reyes had temporarily turned his back on the door, talking with another officer. He spun around as the female officer called his name but not before I whizzed into the room. Morrie's shocked expression did little to faze me as I slammed my hands down on the table.

"Where the fuck is my son?" I screamed at him. His eyes grew wide, his jaw becoming slack as he shook his head. I didn't wait to hear more of his lies. "Don't tell me you don't know where he's at, you son of a bitch. If you've hurt one hair on his head, I swear to God I'll—"

"Lady!" he yelled back at me, cutting short my threat. "I have no idea where your kid is, okay? I don't know anything about this!"

"You are a disgusting liar," I spat at him. "You would do anything to save your own ass now."

"Listen, lady, I swear to you, I have no idea what happened to your boy. I talk a big talk, but I don't know nothing about this. I stay in my apartment most times and don't bother leaving. Everyone around here knows what I done. There's no way I could do anything that they're saying."

"Annabeth," Reyes hissed.

I ignored him, keeping my attention focused on Jenkins. "Why are you asking for a lawyer then? Huh?"

His cheeks flushed red as he looked down at his hands. "I dunno." He shrugged. "My life sucks."

"You're a child molester. You shouldn't even have one," I spat at him.

He glared back at me. "I served my time. Now I can't even walk down the street without someone screaming at me. What kind of life is that? I wasn't gonna turn down the attention."

I chuckled. "You disgusting asshole. You really don't know anything, do you?"

"I know things!" he blurted out.

It was a last-ditch effort to feel of some importance. I could see it now for what it really was and not just a show of his sick mind. Hours had been wasted on the poor blubbering idiot. They should have taken him right back to his miserable apartment, but it wasn't my decision to make. When Gabriel grabbed my arm, I let him pull me from the room and past the now fuming female officer. He slammed the door behind him as I once again flopped into the chair, still positioned near the computer screen.

"What the hell were you thinking? I should have you arrested for that little stunt of yours!" he yelled at me.

"He doesn't know anything," I sobbed, the pain washing across my body.

"I know that it doesn't seem that way, but we are still going to hold him just in case," Reyes said in a soothing tone. "You shouldn't have gone in there though. I'm going to have a ton of paperwork to do now. Plus, the legalities..."

"What are you talking about?"

"Don't you think the defense will use this little

episode of yours to have anything he's said thrown out? It happened in a police station, not really something that we can pretend didn't happen."

"I didn't think about that," I whispered.

"Of course, you didn't!" he yelled. "Because family isn't allowed to be in the room for this very reason. It was a mistake letting you sit in while I talked to Morrie. All I can do now is damage control and hope that they still have enough to book him."

"Gabriel," I stammered. "I didn't know that sort of thing could happen. I'm so sorry. If something happens to my son because of this . . ."

I could feel my chest start to tighten, the signs of a panic attack setting in. I took a deep breath, focusing on counting above everything else. I couldn't have another episode in front of Gabriel. He already thought that I had lost my mind twice before. This time, I had no doubt that he would be done with me once and for all. He was the only link I had to my son's case, and I couldn't lose that.

"Hey," he said softly. "Just take a deep breath."

I shook my head and cleared my throat. "I'm fine, really, I promise. I just can't believe that I was so foolish. I let my emotions get the best of me. Do you think that I've screwed everything up?"

He sighed. "I don't think so, honestly. There is something that Jenkins isn't telling us, but I don't think it has a whole lot to do with the case. For all we know, he's got a stash of illegal porn somewhere."

I shuddered. "Either way, I think I'm ready to get out of here unless you need anything else from me."

"Were you able to look through all the photographs from earlier?"

"I was," I said carefully. "I just don't think it's the same person. I know there are a dozen different ways to explain how sloppy everything was, but I know my kidnapper. Those photos were not his work. He was very careful in everything he did."

"Then I guess there is nothing else that we can do right now. I have a few leads out there right now. One is looking into the van incident that happened earlier."

"You'll let me know when you find out something?" I asked.

"Only if you promise to keep your head on the level next time, okay?" he offered.

I smiled at him. His tone was apologetic but sincere. I knew that he only wanted what was best for me. Someone knocked on the door and my cheeks flushed. I'd been lost in the moment and the sound startled me. Gabriel shot me a sly grin as I jumped in my seat. I straightened my back when I saw the female detective glare at me over Reyes's shoulders.

I didn't need to hear what she was saying to get the gist of the conversation. She was pissed at how Gabriel was handling the situation, no doubt. I couldn't stop a smirk from playing across my lips. For the first time in a very long while, it felt good to be desired by a man and to know I could still make someone jealous. Reyes closed the door.

"Ready to head home?" he asked.

I nodded. "Absolutely."

CHAPTER ELEVEN

As he led me out into the waiting room, I could sense something was on his mind. When we lingered by the door longer than needed, though, I finally had to break the silence.

"Well," I blurted out. "Thanks for everything."

"I was hoping that you'd let me drive you home," he said almost sheepishly.

I flushed instantly. "Look, I think you are a really nice guy and all but—"

"No," he shot in before I could continue. "I just mean that someone followed you here. Plus, you've been through a lot in the last few days and the last few hours. I don't think I could forgive myself if you didn't make it home safe."

"Oh! Right, sure," I quickly agreed. "Yeah, that makes sense. So, should I just leave my car here?"

"I wouldn't want to inconvenience you. I'll drive you home in your car, then I can get an Uber or something from there."

"You'll at least have to let me pay for it."

He grinned and stepped to the side so I could lead the way to my car. "I wouldn't dream of taking the honor away from the city though. They love it when I send in to be reimbursed."

I couldn't help but laugh. "Whatever makes you happy! Second gear likes to stick sometimes. I just can't bring myself to take it to the shop."

"You've kept it in great shape. I take it she belonged to your late husband?"

I smiled sadly and nodded. "A seventy-eight cutlass. He loved this car."

"I can see why. Original paint too?"

"Baby blue, his favorite color."

"I don't blame you one bit for hanging onto it," Gabriel said as he held open the passenger door. He climbed into his side. "I still have the pearl necklace my wife wore on our wedding day. Sometimes, it's okay to hang onto those memories."

"Wow," I said softly.

"Is everything okay?" he asked, looking at me with concern.

I nodded. "Yeah, I just." I took a deep breath. "I've never really talked with anyone who knows what it's like to lose a partner before."

"You haven't tried any support groups?"

"No," I admitted. "it's hard with my social anxiety."

"Well," Gabriel said with a confident grin. "I can be your support group for now. It helps to have someone to talk to. Thank God there aren't too many people who have to understand the pain we've gone through, but it's nice to be able to share. Maybe I can talk you into joining a group or two after we find Gregory."

"You are so confident," I whispered as I watched the traffic and city pass by. "Every day that he's still missing, I feel the depression trying to creep back in."

"I like to have faith," Reyes said absentmindedly. "I just don't feel like Jenkins is our man. He was too comfortable in the police station. Like he missed being part of the movements, but when he saw you, his eyes couldn't lie."

"I know," I muttered. "Thank you for everything that you're doing to help me find him. I don't know if I've told you that yet."

He grinned at me. "I don't know if you have or not, but it doesn't matter one bit. I know that I would be losing my mind if one of my girls were missing."

"You don't talk about them much," I offered.

"I don't like to talk about them while I'm on the job."

"Oh," I said quickly.

"Wait," he blurted out suddenly. "That's not what I meant. I'm happy to tell you about them, really, I am. I just don't normally talk about them. If I do, I start to get worried about my job and leaving them without any parents. It's hard when you're all your kids have."

"I can understand that. I didn't mean to pry," I said.

"Please don't apologize," he said in a warm tone. "It's still hard without their mother, but we are getting into the swing of things. I can't imagine life in ten years with her still gone."

"It gets a little easier. We have a good support system too."

"Do you date?" he asked softly.

My cheeks flushed. "Um, I don't really have the time with working and Gregory's diagnosis. I haven't really missed it much, until now."

"Now?" he said, his eyebrow arching.

I was going to come up with some witty answer, but before I could, I saw his eyes dart to the mirror. He'd been so supportive thus far. It was out of character for him. I looked around the car. It was messy, as was expected with a young boy, but otherwise, there was nothing damning. I could tell that something was distracting him. It wouldn't have caught my attention, but it was the third time in as many minutes that he'd done so.

My heart started to speed up. I wasn't that much of a slob. Something caught the corner of my eye in the passenger mirror. My mouth fell open in shock. There, creeping behind us a few cars, was the same van from earlier.

"That's him, the same man as before."

"I thought it might be. They've been following us for three blocks now."

"So not since the station? Do you think it could be Jenkins?"

"I don't know, but it's possible. They could have cut him loose after we left. If he was parked nearby, then it wouldn't be hard for him to catch up to us."

"Oh, my God," I stammered. "What do we do? Do we call the police?"

Reyes chuckled. "I am the police. Let's make sure it's him first, okay? For all we know, we could both be letting our imaginations get the best of us."

He turned on the blinker and moved over two lanes to exit near the local mall. I could get us home from there, but it would take longer. We both watched with bated breath to see what the van would do. I let out a sigh of relief when it didn't look like they were going to move over and follow us off the highway.

"Shit," hissed Reyes.

My eyes jerked back to the road behind us. In the final seconds before the exit passed by, the van had cut across the busy lanes of traffic to get off on the exit behind us. My confidence and my doubt that they were following us both shattered at once. Instantly, it felt like my heart was going to explode from fear. I could feel my hands shaking but I couldn't focus on them or anything else. Panic was taking control, darkness setting in.

Suddenly, something pulled me back from the brink. A warm sensation on my hand jerked me back to reality. Gabriel had taken my hand, squeezing it with confidence.

"Hey, this is a good thing. Maybe we can find out who is really behind this. Don't worry, we've been training new recruits in defensive driving since the Kennedy assassination."

"That's good to know, I guess."

My attention was still on the van as it followed us, now doing very little to hide the fact. Even though we were driving through a densely populated area, Reyes continued to speed up. He swerved between cars, trying to put some space between us and the other driver. Even with all of his training, the man stalking us seemed determined to run us off the road. Or stay on our tail, at the very least.

He fished around in his pocket and pulled out a radio. "Dispatch, this is detective Reyes, over?"

"What are you doing?" I whispered as we waited for a response.

"I know when I need to ask for a little help. This maniac doesn't know that it's a cop driving you home."

"What if that just makes him angrier and he takes it out on Gregory? I don't think we should risk it. Just get us out of here."

'Dispatch, over,' came a man's voice.

Reyes sighed. "I've got a brown van, delta Shrek oh-nine-oh-one-five out by the Riverview Mall, driving like a maniac. Someone needs to get over there."

I sighed, sitting back in my seat and praying that it didn't make things worse for Gregory.

"There," Gabriel said with confidence. "Now they will come looking for the van but not with their guns blazing. Just a random call to the local police about a bad driver. Could be any number of concerned citizens out here."

"Thanks, I guess," I muttered. My eyes were still trained on the van. "He is getting closer."

"I know. I think he's going to try and run us off the road if he can get close enough."

"What should we do?" I asked in a panic. "I swear to God, he's getting closer."

"That's a very good observation," Reyes muttered, more complimentary than condescending. "Unfortunately, it doesn't look like we are going to be able to shake him. If the station is busy, it could be hours before someone gets out here."

"Jesus, for a crazy driver in the middle of the city?" I snapped.

"There are a lot of crimes in this city and not enough funds for the force. You'd be surprised at the kind of calls we get that we can't always take right away. This town isn't the darling little place it used to be."

"Isn't that the truth," I agreed frantically.

I couldn't take my eyes off the mirror. The van was beyond swerving dangerously now. I couldn't believe what I was seeing with my own eyes. How anyone could blatantly put so many innocent people at risk was beyond me. The fire flared inside me as it dawned on me that he was the reason my son was missing.

"We should trap the son of a bitch, make him tell us where my baby is. He can't be carrying a gun or anything. He didn't use one the other day. Why would he have one now?"

I knew that I was rambling. It was hard to think straight with everything happening at once. Reyes was saying something, but I couldn't focus on him. All I could think about was the man following us. Did he have my son with him? Was there someone he was working with? Reyes shook my arm, jerking me out of the trance I'd been sucked into.

"Hey! I can't lose you right now, okay? I need you to stay focused for me. Can you do that?"

"Of course, I can," I snapped at him unreasonably. "Jesus, I'm not a child. You don't have to treat me like one."

"Easy, now," he said in a calming tone. "You just looked like you were spacing out for a second. Am I not allowed to be worried about you?"

"Not when someone is trying to run us off the road," I told him in a harsh tone.

I couldn't think about what would happen to Gregory if I lost my grip now. Reyes eased off the gas a little and the car following us slowed its pace some, but we were still getting nowhere fast. Every time we tried to lose him, his driving would become erratic and put others at risk. That wasn't blood I wanted on my hands.

"What are we going to do?" I asked him softly.

"We can't shake him, not without risking our own lives," he muttered.

"I don't care about my life, not without Gregory in it. He is my world. If there is a way for us to corner that son of a bitch, then take it."

"That isn't your call to make. Hell, its not even mine!" Gabriel shot back. "I won't put your life in danger to possibly help your son. I know you are scared and worried about him, but now is the not the time to be a martyr, okay?"

I snorted. "Is that what you think I'm doing?"

"No." his tone was calmer. "I think that you are a mother who is worried about her son. We've been playing this game for too long. I didn't want to do this, but we need to call in backup."

"What if they don't get here in time or he gets away? Won't that just make him angry?"

"Annabeth, we just don't have any more options."

For a split second, his eyes left the road and focused on mine. I could see what the decision was doing to him. He didn't like it any more than I did. Suddenly, I was reminded of who Gabriel was outside of the uniform. He, too, had children. I wasn't just putting my life in danger, but I was risking two little girls growing up without a father. My heart ached as it was torn into different directions, but ultimately, I knew what the right decision was.

I nodded my head and whispered softly, "Call them in. Let's get this over with."

Reyes smiled at me, reaching down for his phone before suddenly jerking the car to a stop.

"What are you doing?" I asked, my heart racing as the van inched closer to us in the mirror.

"Son of a bitch," he muttered.

I glanced in front of us and my stomach dropped to the floor. "That son of a bitch."

"I don't think trapping him is an option anymore."

The cement barricade in front of us blocked us in from three sides. The van was quickly making the square complete. There was no way we were going to get out, and it would be a miracle if the police made it to our aid in time.

"No," I said in a dry tone. "He got to us first."

CHAPTER TWELVE

"Oh, my God. Oh, my God. Oh, my God," I heaved under my breath.

"Just take it easy," Gabriel said quickly as he worked.

I focused on what he was doing, watching him work while I kept one eye trained on the van. So far, it hadn't moved, its driver still sitting behind the wheel in a dark hood. There was no need for me to see his face. Something inside me clicked, and I knew that it was the same bastard who'd taken my son. Rage flooded my body as I jerked on the seatbelt, trying desperately to free myself.

"What the hell do you think you're doing?" Gabriel hissed. "Don't even think about moving or I will throw your ass in prison!"

My heart raced in trepidation. "But my son."

"Is going to be fine, but not if his mother is dead when he comes back. You need to stay here and trust me."

"What are you going to do?"

From behind his back, he produced a black gun. It sent a shiver of fear through my spine. I never liked the idea of guns, and the current situation was doing little to ease my fears. Gabriel saw the look in my eyes and smiled softly. He slipped the gun into his other hand and slid the free one over to mine. I knew that he was taking his time to make sure I was okay.

"I am going to be right back. While I'm gone, though, I need you to call the police station for me, okay? All you need to do is let them know I'm here with you and I need immediate backup. Can you do that for me?"

I was shaking as I nodded my head. He slipped his hand away, sliding the phone into my palm before giving me one more confident smile. I didn't want to let go of his hand, still wrapped around his phone. The touch was delicate and informal, but I still couldn't let him go. I knew how dangerous the man waiting for him outside was. There was no stopping him. I had to remember the task at hand.

Quickly dialing the precinct on his phone, I was

connected with a familiar female voice. "Officer Haden, what's your emergency?"

"You!" I blurted out, surely sounding like a madman. "Oh, my God, this is Annabeth, from earlier? Gabriel needs your help right away!"

"Ma'am, I need you to calm down. Tell me what's going on."

"Jesus, we don't have time for this. Detective Reyes is in danger at the mall! The man who has my son cornered us here! The brown van?" I rushed to fill in the missing details.

"Annabeth, I need you to listen to me very carefully. Can you see the detective now?"

"Yes. He's approaching the passenger side of the van now. He's got his gun drawn. Oh, my God, please, can you send someone? What if that maniac has a gun after all?"

"I have cars on the way, but I need you to stay on the line with me. Can you do that? What's happening now?"

"Um," I tried to focus. "He's almost to the window. I can't see the driver's face but I just know it's him. The windows are tinted too dark."

"Just tell me what happens, okay? It's very important that you stay on the line with me."

My heart pounded. "Something's happening." The

window started to move. "The driver is rolling down the window. He's got something!"

I watched in horror as Gabriel swung around. I couldn't see anything with him standing in front of me, but I could hear him yelling at the driver to step out of the vehicle. In a split second, Reyes dove to the side, and I jumped, letting out a terrified scream as a single bullet pierced the car and flew past me, shattering glass as it went.

"Annabeth!" Hayden yelled on the phone. "Shots fired, shots fired," she yelled at someone else in the station. "Annabeth, what's happening? You've got to be my eyes out there. Is Detective Reyes wounded?"

My whole body was shaking as I peeked again out the driver's window. Reyes was looking right at me, motioning for me to get down. The mystery driver was swinging the weapon around now like a maniac. Gabriel again ordered the man to put down his weapon, identifying himself as the police, but the driver didn't seem to care. I could see Gabriel was thinking about his next move.

In the distance, wailing sirens started to approach us. I couldn't take my eyes off Gabriel, though, not even when the van lurched into gear and squealed away from us. Reyes was back at the door in a matter of seconds, gunning my car's engine and giving chase to the van. It was exactly what I would have done in that situation. I just wanted to find Gregory.

"Where is he going?" I stammered. "Are you hurt?"

Reyes shook his head, noticing the phone sitting between us as he quickly grabbed it. "Hayden?" he said quickly. "We are headed south on Sycamore. See if you can't get one of the other guys to head him off. We'll trap him. There is construction up here that he won't be able to get around."

The woman on the other end started to argue with him. I could see his free hand tighten around the wheel as she did. With a rather unflattering scoff, Reyes ended the call by hanging up on her. I could tell that he was angry and that it would do me no good to try and find out what he was really thinking. We had to keep our minds focused on the man in front of us.

"What the hell happened out there?" I finally asked.

"That bastard was trying to kill me. I don't think he planned on shooting at you," he said. His gaze was locked on the van as it drove like a madman was behind the wheel. "He is going to get himself or all three of us killed if he doesn't slow down up here. That bridge isn't finished."

"It doesn't look like he's slowing down. Did you get a good look at him?"

"No," he growled in an angry tone. "Son of a bitch was wearing some kind of ski mask too. I'm not going to let him get away though."

"Please, Reyes," I whispered, my fear now reaching a pinnacle as the unpaved road became more dangerous.

Crews working on the road dove out of the way as the van continued down the dangerous path. My little car wasn't built to take so much, and it started to lurch, the 'check engine' light flashing as we bottomed out on the road. The van, far more rugged than it looked on the outside, continued forward without stopping.

"You are letting him get away!" I blurted out.

"I can't put your life at risk and keep following him. Either he or us will end up dead if I do."

"Then kill the son of a bitch!" I snapped.

"How is that going to help us find Gregory? What if he left him in the care of someone else with orders in case he got caught?"

I sobbed. "I didn't think about that. I just can't believe how close we were to catching him, and now it's gone, our only hope of finding Gregory is gone."

"Hey," he said softly. "Don't think like that, okay? We are going to get him, and this wasn't for nothing. Now we know that it's not a random occurrence."

"What are you talking about?"

"He is after you. He wants you."

"I already knew that," I muttered in discontent.

"Listen, I'm going to get you home, then get back to the precinct while the details are still fresh in my memory. Are you going to be okay?"

I nodded. "I always am. Please, just take me home."

"You've got it," he said, putting the car in reverse and giving up the chase.

I hated that my son's captor was still free to go back to Gregory and take out his anger on my poor sweet boy. Somewhere deep inside, though, I knew that Reyes was right. There was nothing more we could do right now. The police had all the van information, and they would be watching the roads carefully to make sure that he didn't slip by. If nothing else, we'd confirmed that my son's kidnapper would stop at nothing to make this even more personal.

As we drove through the city back to my house, it all felt strangely normal to be next to him. Even after everything we'd just been through, Reyes seemed cool and collected. I wanted to keep him next to me all the time. The soothing nature of his personality was like a drug I was quickly getting hooked onto. My house came into view after twenty minutes of silent driving. I saw my mother's car, and to my shock, Jacob's pickup truck.

"Great," Reyes muttered. "Boy, he watches you like a hawk, doesn't he?"

"He's probably just checking on my mom. Believe it or not, they've known each other a very long time. They may act like they hate each other, but deep down, I think there is a bond."

"I don't know why anyone would want to bond with him. He's got a short fuse and a bad temper."

"Please, let's not start in on this again. He's here, though. Shouldn't that take him off the suspect list?"

"Not in my mind, sorry. There is something off about that man, and I'm going to figure out what it is."

"Does it have to be today? I just want to go lie down. This whole afternoon has been a rollercoaster and I'm ready to get off."

His eyes softened as he nodded his head and put the car in park. "Of course."

"I feel bad that you don't have a car here."

"Actually . . ." He shuffled his feet a little. "My partner is picking me up so we can go back over the scene, but she won't be here for a few minutes. If it's okay, I'd like to talk to your mom too. She was pretty distraught when we spoke at the hospital. I'm hoping a little time and space have eased her mind some."

"Good luck," I muttered. "She's been pretty chilly toward me since this whole thing happened."

"There is something else that I need to talk to you

about. When I was on the phone with Hayden, she let me know that they're releasing Jenkins."

"What?" I asked. "How can they let that pedophile go after what he said in the interrogation room?"

"He didn't outright admit to anything, and his lawyer basically laughed off the charges when they found out you stormed in."

"Oh, my God," I gasped. "So, he is back on the street and it's my fault? How could this get any worse?"

"Don't beat yourself up. I still don't think he's very involved in the case, if he's involved at all, but this way, we can put a couple of guys on him and watch him. Sometimes, suspects break open the case for you without ever knowing it. Either way, he's back on our radar now and won't be slipping through the cracks again."

"I guess something good came out of all of this then. Ready?" I asked him, looking up at my house.

"Ready as I'll ever be," he said.

I hid the laughter that was rising up in my chest. He looked like a teen boyfriend going to meet a terrifying parent for the first time. I liked the way he looked, a little nervous but still confident that he knew what he was doing. My mother would give him a run for his money. With Jacob there, I would just be happy if we all made it out relatively unscathed. I couldn't understand why Jacob hated Reyes so much when he was only trying to find my son.

As we made our way up the walkway and onto the porch, I could hear voices talking heatedly inside. Though I didn't know what they were saying, I had to assume that nothing good could come from the two of them left alone and fighting. I turned the knob, but the door was locked. For a second, I fumbled with my keys until Reyes took them from me and gently slid the key into the lock. I flushed a deep red at his closeness and whispered a 'thanks.'

"Anytime," he whispered back.

Our eyes locked, the heat between us growing more intense with every moment we spent in close quarters with each other. I would have been happy to stand on the porch with him all night, had it not been for my missing son and the approaching footsteps. Jacob jerked open the door, looking over the scene that he'd just witnessed. He was flushed red, beads of sweat dripping down his speckled brow and onto his pressed white shirt.

"Jacob!" I said, trying to muster up any kind of excitement at seeing him. It continued to elude me. "I was just getting ready to give you a call."

An awkward silence filled the air as Jacob tried to stare down Gabriel. Though he outweighed him by at least fifty pounds, Jacob would never win over the police officer in a combat situation. He didn't seem to get the memo, though, as his chest puffed out and he took a step closer to the detective.

"Who the hell do you think you are?" Jacob hissed at him.

Gabriel laughed at Jacob's attempt at a threat. It was going to be a long afternoon after all.

CHAPTER THIRTEEN

Gabriel, much to his credit, took the attempt at hostility in stride. He didn't seem nearly as flustered by the confrontation as I felt. I swallowed hard, waiting for Gabriel to say something.

"Well, my name is Detective Reyes. I'm helping with Annabeth's case."

"I know who you are. Don't talk to me like I'm an idiot. Why are you here?" Jacob demanded. Before Gabriel could respond, Jacob turned his attention and anger toward me. "So, this is why you didn't call me back? You were with him."

"He was just driving me home," I said quickly as I shoved my way past him.

Mom was still sitting at the kitchen table. She'd made no effort to get up when she saw it was just me at the door. I hated the tension in our house. I hated that she resented me for Tom's injuries. More than anything, I wished I could take back the entire situation and flee the state with Gregory. We never would have looked back if I'd only known the pain and heartache that my presence there would bring her.

"Mom," I said in a monotone. "How was work? Short day?"

"Am I not allowed to come home and have a cup of coffee?"

"It just seems a little out of character for you in the middle of the day. Especially with Jacob."

"Jacob and I go way back, but you probably don't remember that."

"No," I muttered as I sat down. "I do. I just don't ever remember you two spending time together."

"And I don't remember you telling me you were dating a cop," she snapped.

I rolled my eyes, my attention now split between my mother and Jacob, who I knew was listening to every word I was saying, even if he didn't appear so. The already tense situation was heightened by the rush of testosterone in the room. It was Gabriel who finally broke the silence, stepping around Jacob and into the house. I could see how much it drove Jacob mad, and a smug smile played on my lips, though I tried to hide it.

"Ma'am," Reyes started as he approached my

mother. "I was hoping you'd have a second to talk. How is your son doing?"

"I've already told you people everything I know. I don't see why you keep harassing my family."

"Mom," I snapped. "He saved my life today when that maniac was following me!"

She rolled her eyes. "Oh, please, don't you think you are being a little dramatic?"

"No, mother." I glared at her. "The man shot out my window."

"How do you know that he was trying to kill you?" Jacob interrupted.

"Because he shot at me! How hard is that for you people to understand!" I screamed.

"Annabeth," Gabriel said in a soothing tone.

I took a deep breath, reminding myself that I didn't need to lose my temper over little things. There were much bigger pictures that we needed to focus on.

"Ma'am?" Reyes pressed.

Mom rolled her eyes. "Oh, fine, if I have to."

She stood up with a dramatic flourish and stormed into the kitchen, smacking her leg as if she was calling for a dog to follow her. I wanted to flick her in the forehead for being so disrespectful to the law. It didn't matter the circumstances. There were certain people you just owed respect to. Especially when it was someone who was trying to help find your grandson and who saved your daughter's life. I sighed, looking down at my hands as I tried to remind myself that she was in pain too.

"So now you are ditching me for cops?" Jacob grumbled from behind me.

I sighed. "I wasn't ditching you for anyone. God, what is wrong with you people? After the police station, he offered to drive me home. I was a little emotional, to say the least."

"Then you should have called me."

"There was no reason to. Gab—" I clenched my jaw. "Detective Reyes was there and offered. It was a good thing he did, too, because that maniac who took Gregory tried to off us!"

"Annabeth, you should have called me. I could have kept you a lot safer than that scrawny officer. You know he's just trying to get into your pants, right?"

"Jesus, Jacob, don't you have any class? It was a ride home, and one which I was grateful for. What are you doing here, anyway? Since when do you and my mother have long talks while I'm gone?"

"Since when do you go running around and turning off your phone? I was worried about you. I came over here to make sure that you were okay. It wasn't until your mother told me you messaged her that I was finally able to take a deep breath again."

"Well, you shouldn't always be worrying about me.

I'm a grown woman. I don't need a babysitter."

"I hope you don't think of me as a babysitter, just a concerned friend who knows what a hard time you are having right now. I guess I just wanted a firsthand update on what the police were doing to find Gregory."

"Well, now you have it," I snapped.

I felt him tense behind me and moved around in the seat so my back wasn't to him. I hated not being able to see the people I was talking to. It was a latent fear stemming from my own kidnapping. When Gregory came home, he would have so many of the same problems as me. I shuddered and squeezed my eyes shut, trying not to think about the worst possible outcome. Jacob reached out and squeezed my shoulder. Instinctively, I jerked away from him and sprang to my feet.

"Do not touch me," I hissed in a harsher tone than intended.

His face flushed red, rage apparent underneath his thin exterior. My back was to the door when my mother and Gabriel, now chatting like old friends, appeared behind me. They could sense the tension in the room. Gabriel lightly touched my arm to get my attention. The sensation didn't make me jump though. I looked at him and smiled, nodding my head in reassurance that I was fine.

"You've got to be kidding me," Jacob hissed. He

was now seeing red.

"Is there a problem here?" Gabriel asked, his gaze leveled on Jacob but his hand still lightly touching my arm.

"No," I quickly replied. "I think I've had enough excitement for one day, though, if you'll excuse me."

"Perfect timing," Gabriel said with his easy smile. "Hayden is waiting for me outside."

"That your girlfriend?" Jacob spat out.

Gabriel wasn't fazed. "My partner, when I need one, of course. I prefer to work alone on most cases, but I want to make sure Annabeth and Gregory are getting the best the station has to offer right now."

Jacob rolled his eyes. "If you'd done your job the first time, this never would have happened."

"Well, I wasn't with the force at that time, but since you seem to be older, maybe you'd like to come down to the station and fill in some details."

"Are you threatening me?" Jacob snapped, stepping closer to Gabriel.

Reyes looked amused but not concerned. "Of course not. You just seem very involved in the case. I thought you could offer some extra insight."

"If it will keep you away from Annabeth, then I'll do whatever you want."

"Come now, we are working on a missing persons case. Even if I could cut Annabeth out of the loop, I would never do it. She has a right to the information far more than you do."

"All you are doing is dredging up bad memories and making her life hell. Do you think you're a bigger man for that?" snapped Jacob.

"Jacob!" I said in shock. "This needs to stop right now. Gabriel, I'll talk with you soon, but I think it's best if you leave."

He smiled at me, squeezing my arm gently, though I knew it was more to irritate Jacob than for my own benefit. It didn't matter. Either way, his touch on my skin felt right, almost natural. I walked him back to the front door and smiled as he waved at me from the car. He was a good man, that much I knew to be true. I could count the people I trusted on one hand, and he was now one of them.

I turned around to see my mother heading back to the kitchen. Part of me wanted to beg her to stay in the room, but I knew it was a lost cause. She and Jacob had worked out whatever differences they had and now it was my turn. At some point, I knew that we were going to have to talk about how she felt toward me, but for now, I was content to let Jacob have the brunt end of my anger.

"What the hell was that?" I snapped at him right away. "Gabriel has done nothing but help me out these last few days. You have no right to be so rude to him!"

"I don't like the way he looks at you or the way he touches you! I would never get away with doing something like that!"

"Well, maybe it's okay when he does it. Have you ever stopped to think about that?"

"Wow." His eyes grew wide before darkening. "I never thought that you would be the type to go screwing around while your son was missing."

"Fuck you," I blurted out before I could stop myself.

Jacob sucked in a sharp breath, his cheeks flaming red again. "What did you just say?"

"Argh!" I yelled in frustration. "Why are you even here? Jesus, Jacob, it's like everywhere I look, you are right there, giving me a hard time. Of course, I'm not sleeping with him! That's all you ever think about, whether I'm screwing around with someone. Well guess what? It's none of your damn business who is in my personal life."

"That's because until you met that prick with a badge, you didn't have a personal life! It's a little strange that Gregory goes missing and suddenly, you are cuddle buddies with a cop."

"Do you even hear how crazy you sound? Acting like this is some master plot of Gabriel's? God, have you lost your mind?"

"If I have, it's because of you and the way you lead

people on."

"Jeeze, what are you talking about now?"

"I thought we were getting coffee after your meeting with the pig, and you bailed on me, again. I guess I shouldn't be too surprised."

"I didn't bail on you, asshole. I was helping them to eliminate a suspect. Isn't that what this is all about? Finding Gregory? For someone who acts like they are so concerned, you sure do have your priorities mixed up. God, you are more worried about who I'm sleeping with than finding my son."

His eyes widened, his mouth dropping open. "So, you are sleeping with him?"

I wanted to tell him 'yes', that we were having a wild, torrid affair instead of looking for my son, who was the only important man in my life. But I couldn't get the lie to form on my lips. I didn't want to run Gabriel's name through the mud just because I was fighting with a man who'd been part of my life for over a decade. Instead, I childishly shrugged my shoulders, not committing to one single answer.

"I knew it. I'll fucking kill him," he hissed.

"Oh, for the love of God," I said as I rolled my eyes. "Not that it's any of your business, but no, we are not sleeping together. When I told you our relationship was just professional, I meant it."

"But you let him touch you," Jacob seethed.

I shrugged. "It's not really something I can control. The first time he did it, I wasn't freaked out at all."

"Yeah? How many other men can touch you like that? Or am I special in your disgust?"

"Please, Jacob, can we not do this again right now? It's been a long day and I'm tired of fighting with you and for my life. I've been shot at, my son is still missing, and you are being a really lousy friend."

He took a deep breath and nodded his head. "Yeah. I guess you are right. I'm just so worried about you. Do you want me to stay here for a while so you can rest without worrying about people breaking in?"

I shook my head. "Mom is done at work, and she doesn't go to the hospital for a few hours, so I'm going to sleep then ride in with her."

"Well," he said, sounding like a broken little boy. "If you change your mind, let me know. You know I only want what's best for you."

"I know," I assured him.

Jacob made his way to the door and I let him go. He was sulking like a child, but I didn't have it left inside me to coddle him. At some point, I might want to start dating again, and it would do him well to remember that he was a friend and nothing more. Something told me that he wasn't going to take the news lying down. I wasn't even sure anymore if he was there for me or for the prospect of conquering me.

CHAPTER FOURTEEN

The door slammed behind him, making me jump a little as my mother came back into the dining room. She looked around the otherwise empty house and sat down at the table.

"Did everyone leave?" my mom asked.

I nodded. "Yeah, Detective Reyes went to follow leads and Jacob is having a temper tantrum again."

She chuckled and shook her head. "He does have a bit of a short temper."

"How well do you know Jacob? I didn't think you two were friends. I mean, he's always been my friend. I didn't think you two had much of a relationship."

She sighed. "We aren't really close, I admit that. I guess extreme circumstances bring people together."

I suppose when terrible things happen, you look to

whoever is willing to help. Jacob wasn't being very helpful to me at the moment, but he was just about all I had. When you spend most of your adult life holed up at home, it doesn't leave a lot of opportunity to make new friends. So, I did my best to keep any of the old ones I had. Unfortunately, when you're afraid to leave the house, it's easy to cancel lunch dates and nights out. People could only be understanding and patient for so long.

"We've reached rock-bottom," I said morosely. "My car is being followed and the old neighbor kid is stopping over for coffee and a chat. You know, if you wanted to talk to someone who's actually helpful with these things, you could see a therapist. Mine has been very beneficial."

My mom shook her head. "There aren't enough hours in the day. I have to go to work and visit your brother. If I'm going to spend an hour or two to decompress, then I'd like to do it in the privacy of my own home. Besides, I'd rather talk to someone who knows me than a stranger with a notepad."

I wasn't going to argue the point any further. I decided to change the subject and go back to Jacob.

"So, you've known Jacob for as long as I have. Has he always been this protective, or has he reached a whole new level?"

"I've noticed," she replied, rubbing her temples. "I

don't always know if he's the best choice of a friend to have by your side at this particular moment."

"He's all I've got," I replied.

"I guess." My mom sighed. "No, I think he's being a little more overbearing than usual. He's a nice enough guy, but he needs to take it down a notch."

"But you think he's always been a little high-strung?"

My mom let out a laugh like a bark. "I always thought it was a little strange that a boy his age would ever have anything to do with a little girl. You were only in middle school when we moved next door to his parents. But, I got to know his parents over the years and they're great people. It kind of made me feel like it was okay to let you two hang out."

"You've never told me this before," I said, surprised by this revelation. "I didn't know that you had any doubts about our friendship."

"It's a mother's job," she said shortly. "I may not have told you that I was looking into anyone you spent time with as a kid, but I certainly did my research. Remember that boy I forbade you to date in high school?"

"John Moriarty?"

"I heard that he had a reputation for getting a little too handsy with other girls. I wasn't going to let my daughter earn a bad reputation because of him."

I chuckled to myself. Perhaps I didn't give my mom enough credit.

"Did Jacob give you reason to vet him? I just remember one day I was playing in the yard and he was there."

"I remember that day well. You were rollerblading around the driveway and I was in the kitchen. I looked out the window to see some high school boy talking to you. I nearly stormed out right that moment to yell at him."

"Did he do something?" I gulped.

"No, no, nothing like that. I just thought it seemed strange that he would want anything to do with you. No offense, of course."

"None taken," I said dryly. I guess I had never really thought about the origin of my friendship with Jacob. We lost contact with each other over the years, but after Greg was killed, he came back into my life. It was a blessing, too. At that time, the only thing I needed was someone who would sit with me as I shook with fear and didn't judge me because I was an emotional wreck. At my current age, it didn't seem strange that I was friends with a slightly older man. After a certain point, age didn't mean much. But as a child, I could see where my friendship with an older guy would give my mom pause.

"So," I said, clearing my throat, "what did you do to check him out?"

My mom furrowed her brow, trying to remember back a decade or so. "Well, I got to know his parents. Usually, if the parents check out, the kid checks out too. If I had walked over there and the house was a mess and his mom was rude to me, then I would have problems."

"Seems a little judgmental," I said.

"You have a kid of your own," she said, narrowing her eyes at me. "Call me prejudiced, but you use whatever resources you have to keep your kid safe."

I swallowed hard. I know she probably didn't mean to come off as harsh, but since my child was currently in harm's way, it felt as though she was trying to make a point. I felt helpless enough as it was. I wanted to do more to find my son, but the police made it clear that I would only get in their way. So, I had to sit and make small talk with my mother while the police worked to find Gregory.

"I guess you're right," I grumbled.

"Still, we didn't like the idea of an older boy hanging around our daughter, no matter how good his parents were. Do you remember me trying to convince you to spend more time with people your own age?"

"Vaguely," I said, biting the inside of my cheek. "I didn't know that was because you didn't trust Jacob."

She nodded. "We even tried to talk to Jacob about spending time with people his age. He wasn't very happy when I told him that."

I raised my eyebrows. "I didn't know you talked to him about me. He's never brought that up before."

"Not surprised. He was a little embarrassed."

I felt guilty. It couldn't have been easy for Jacob to hear that. He had a bit of a fragile ego—just typical guy stuff.

"Looking back, I kind of feel bad for him," I admitted. "Maybe he didn't have a lot of friends and I was willing to talk to him."

I remember thinking it was pretty cool to have a male friend who was more mature than the guys in my class. Even then, I admired how intelligent Jacob was. In fact, he became quite the influence in my life. If I hadn't tried to learn things to impress him, I would have never studied Computer Science. He was still ahead of me in terms of knowledge, and probably would always be, but I had made a name for myself in the programming world. My work was rarely consistent, but it was enough to live on.

"No, I suppose he didn't. He seemed like the kind of kid who would be too easy to pick on. He was kind of a know-it-all, and those types don't typically do well in school. Of course, you were a very kind and naïve kid, so you were just interested in what he had to say.

Of course it wouldn't annoy you to be told things you might already know, because you didn't. Though I appreciated the fact that you had a friend to tutor you through Algebra so I didn't have to. Still, he wasn't a perfect angel."

I frowned. "What do you mean?"

"He doted on you, but he could be bossy and jealous. One time, he came to the door and you weren't home. He asked what you were up to and I told him that you were at a school dance. His face turned bright red and he pitched a little tantrum on the front step."

"What did you do?" I asked, surprised by this behavior. The Jacob of my childhood had perhaps been a little protective, but not controlling.

"I set him straight the moment I could even comprehend what was going on. I told him to knock that possessive crap off right that instant. He sulked away and hadn't been outwardly controlling since —until now."

I nibbled on a hangnail. I had a sneaking suspicion that I knew exactly what she was talking about. I didn't want to admit that she was right about how crazy he had been acting lately. If I did, it would be as if she was right to want to keep us apart. He was the closest friend I had, and I didn't want her convincing me that I shouldn't allow him to support me through a difficult time.

Though he was starting to annoy me by his persistent attempts to be more than a friend, I didn't want to lose him. He was clearly just rattled by everything that had happened and afraid to lose me. I understood his concern, but I couldn't handle his panic when I had so much of mine to deal with. After all, he wasn't the one with a missing child.

"I'm just worried he's going to have another freak-out," my mom said pointedly.

I scowled. I didn't like when people spoke of mental health crises so crassly. I had dealt with enough of my own. That being said, she had a point.

When I moved away from home to go to college, Jacob was bereft. After he graduated from high school, he went to community college and lived at home. In fact, he was almost exclusively self-taught. But he never really moved away from his parents' house until they packed up and bought a small condo in Boca Raton.

Anyway, when I left for college, Jacob had a breakdown. Everyone said that it was because I was leaving him, but it seemed like a convenient answer to a complicated problem. In fact, it got so bad that he had to be hospitalized in a psychiatric unit for a while. I was already moved into my dorm when I heard the news. I tried to come home, but my mom convinced me to stay away. I couldn't put my life on hold because of him. I felt bad about not visiting him right away, but it was probably best for his recovery.

Honestly, I was having a hard time remembering much about Jacob. After I was attacked, my long-term memory took a hit. I could remember a lot of things, like my high school graduation and my wedding day. But the events that were less significant were easily lost.

The doctors told me that I would regain some memories over time, but they prepared me for the fact that my brain won't always work the way it used to. My therapist told me that some memories might be in there, but I'm purposefully blocking them out to protect myself. The thought of having horrible memories terrifies me. But sometimes, I wish I had some of my memories from before one of the many times I was attacked by my tormentor.

I wish I had more memories of my son. There have been times where he's brought up something we did together, but I couldn't quite remember. His memory was impeccable, though, so it was silly to be so upset about forgetting what I made him for breakfast on September third. By the way, it was slightly burned toast with butter and marmalade.

"Can you tell me about that?" I asked sheepishly.

Mom sighed. "You don't remember that, do you?"

I hated to admit it, but she was right. My memories

of Jacob's hospitalization were fuzzy. I mostly remember what I was told later on when the subject came up.

"He came over to talk to you. He must have forgotten that you were going to college or hoping that you'd change your mind. I think he was in denial. Anyway, I told him that you were gone. It was like his brain was a computer and it melted. He just stood there, like he didn't know who he was. Then, he started yelling."

"About what?"

"All sorts of things. Most of them didn't make sense. I had to call the police. I didn't want to, but I was freaked out. He's not a small guy—I didn't know what he was going to do."

"You thought he was going to hurt you?"

She frowned. "Not necessarily. He was clearly having some kind of episode. I was frightened, and I didn't want a screaming kid on my lawn. He obviously needed medical attention and his parents weren't around."

I shook my head. I couldn't help but have a little sympathy for him. I know there were several times after my attack that I froze up at the grocery store or in line at the bank because my mind took me to a dark place.

"I know I told you that I visited him in the hospital, but that was just to keep you from coming home. I didn't want to see him—I mean, he was just the strange neighbor kid who had a thing for my daughter. For the most part, he was really good to you, but I didn't want you to rush back here every time he had a tantrum."

"It doesn't sound like a tantrum," I said sternly.

"You know what I mean. Anyway, he was there for a while. I'm sure he was put on medication of some kind and talked to a therapist about whatever it was that caused the episode."

"Did he seem better after he got home?" I asked, angry at myself for not really remembering what became of Jacob.

She shook her head. "Goodness, I have no idea. Before, I used to see him around every once in a while. After he got home, he stayed there. He didn't come over to chat and see how you were doing. I think that's what caused him to move out of his parents' house for good."

"That was probably good for him," I thought, especially considering the fact that I was still living with my parent. If I were healthy enough to live on my own, I'm sure it would be good for my independence.

"I'm sure it was," she agreed. "He seems a lot better. But after this second attack, he's been really squirrely. I told him that I wanted him to cool down.

He really cares about you, and there's no telling what he would do."

"What do you think he'd do?" I asked, feeling concerned.

"No clue with that one," she said. "I don't think it's a good idea for him to be meddling with the police. If he wanted to do their job, then he should join the force. If he wants to help pass out flyers or search the rural parts of town, then that's fine. I just don't think he should be butting into the investigation. He's acting like he's going to find the freak who did this to my family and rip him limb from limb. It's a nice sentiment, but have you seen him? I don't think he does much more than sit in his basement all day."

I ignored the comment about his physique and tried to imagine Jacob killing my attacker. It would be nice to finally have some justice for my family, have my baby back in my arms, and have the nightmare end, but I didn't want Jacob to be the one to do it.

Not only would he somehow manage to bungle the whole operation, but I didn't want to feel like I owed him anything. This wasn't a love story where he would bring my son back and I would decide that I loved Jacob after all. In fact, the thought about being romantic with anyone, let alone Jacob, made my stomach squirm. It was not the time to be thinking of such things. I had much more pressing matters to attend to. My son was missing, my brother was fighting for his life, and I was dealing with the effects of another concussion. I didn't need any more distractions.

"Why now?" my mom asked, her blue eyes staring at me. "He stayed away for so long. Suddenly, he's back and wants to be by your side at all hours of the day. Something doesn't add up."

I shrugged. "I think he wants me to fall in love with him."

Once the words left my mouth, I regretted saying anything at all. I had always hated talking about my relationships with my mom. I didn't want her jumping to conclusions where there were none.

"And?" she asked, raising her thin eyebrows at me.

"And there's nothing to it," I said, getting up from my seat. "I hope he eventually realizes that we're never going to be anything more than friends. Am I manipulating him into helping me by allowing him to stick around?"

"I don't know, and I don't really care," my mom replied. "If he's going to help us in some way, then it doesn't really matter what he thinks is going to happen afterward. Just try and keep him from ruining the investigation with his hotheadedness."

"I'll try," I said dryly, walking toward the stairs. "I'm going to bed."

"Take it easy on the medicine," my mom warned. "You can get addicted to sleeping pills."

"I'm aware," I replied. "I'm not using them right now."

I walked up to my room, closed the door, and unscrewed the cap to the orange prescription bottle. Fishing one little pill out of the bottle, I popped it on my tongue and washed it down with a swig of water. I understood my mother's concern as a nurse, so I didn't want to have to explain to her that I would not be able to sleep without the drugs. Besides, it wasn't as though I was popping pills to get high on a regular basis. I just needed a little help falling asleep.

I found one of Gregory's Legos in my bed and a wave of grief washed over me. As a mother, I had one job. I failed to protect my son and my brother was hurt in the process. He was such a special boy, and my heart broke to think of how scared he must have been when he realized that he was in trouble. The world was already a difficult place for him to understand, and being torn away from everything he had ever known had to be unbearable for him. I just hoped that he was untouched. I couldn't even get my mind to allow for the possibility of anything else.

After a particularly bad bout of anxiety, I had a therapist tell me that if I couldn't sleep because I was worried about something, I should just allow myself some time to stop thinking about whatever was troubling me until morning. There was nothing I could do for my son at this hour, and certainly nothing I could do if I wasn't well rested. I needed to stay sharp for my son. So, after blinking out a few tears, I searched my mind for something less horrifying.

My mind landed on Jacob and how strange he was acting. The last time I told him that I didn't want to date him, he seemed downright angry about it. I understood that tensions were running high, but he didn't have the right to be angry about my choices. In fact, I was annoyed that he would bring something like that up at a time like this. It was inappropriate and weird. He had always been old-fashioned in his way of thinking about women, but this was too much, even for Jacob. I just wished he didn't know me so well so I could use the excuse that I was married. The wedding ring that I occasionally wore around my finger didn't fool him.

After a few hours of trying to keep my mind occupied on lesser horrors, I managed to drift off, aided by the little pill. As my brain became fuzzy, I let out a long exhale of relief. Now, I would be given a brief reprieve from the trauma that surrounded every waking moment.

CHAPTER FIFTEEN

I felt some of the fog leave my head and cracked my eyes open to reveal darkness. I stood up and my heart started racing as I smelled the familiar musty scent of the location of my darkest moments. I reached my hands out, terrified of what I was about to find. Sure enough, my fingertips came into contact with cool stone walls. I was back in the maze.

Strangely enough, my first reaction was relief. If I could navigate the maze, I would be able to retrieve my son. He was certainly in here somewhere, lost and afraid. When I listened hard, I swore I could hear him calling out to me.

My feet felt unbearably heavy when I tried to walk. The ground felt soft under my shoes, as if I were walking on moss or mud. I squinted my eyes, trying to adjust to the darkness, but it was of no use. I was completely blind in the maze.

I took a step forward, both hands out in front of me. Suddenly, I heard a soft whimper coming from somewhere in the room. I listened hard, realizing that the brick walls were creating an echo effect in the room. I couldn't quite pinpoint where the cries were coming from, only that they were coming from my son.

"Gregory!" I cried along with him. "Where are you?"

He didn't answer but just continued to cry. My heart began to pound as my fingers scraped against the wall, searching for my next turn.

"Where are you?" I begged. "Help Mommy find you, Gregory!"

"Help me!" he wailed, finally able to verbalize his fear.

"Tell me where you are!"

More wails. Gregory was a very intelligent boy, but he often had troubles communicating. Plus, he was so young that it was hard for him to understand his situation. He had never been prepared for this kind of experience—no kid should have to be. But, because I spent so much time coaching him on how to act in certain social settings, I felt as though I did him a disservice by not really instructing him about what to do if someone wanted to cause him harm.

Gregory was a trusting kid who took things at face value. If someone told him that they wanted him to go over to their house to work on a fun project, he'd go without a second guess. When he was in the first grade, I had to sit down and tell him how dangerous it was to get into a stranger's car because he tried to catch a ride home with a random guy when I was just a few minutes late to pick him up. I don't think the message really stuck with him, though.

I wanted to shield him from the world because no child should be burdened with everyday horrors. But at the same time, I worried that I was going to make it harder for him to understand truly dangerous situations. So, I did my best to educate him on right and wrong without getting into too much detail and prayed that no one would ever try to take advantage of a disabled kid. I didn't want to tell him too much and add a lifetime of anxiety to his Asperger's. He had been doing so well, and I didn't want to make life any harder for him.

Suddenly, his cries grew louder and more frantic. I dropped to my knees and crawled on the floor, trying to find anything that could help me. Finally, my fingers wrapped around a plastic cylinder. With a flick of the switch, the flimsy flashlight illuminated the foot of space in front of me with its dim light.

I still couldn't see anything in front of me, but at

least I would be able to tell if something was about to pop out at me. I continued along the wall, searching for my son. At one point, I even pointed the light toward the ceiling in case the sounds were coming from above. I even shuffled my feet around, just in case Gregory happened to be beneath me.

"Turn on the freaking lights!" I roared at our captor. I was becoming increasingly frustrated in my search and didn't want to play along anymore. I was so close to having my baby in my arms and I didn't want to wait a second longer. "Just let us go."

He didn't respond. For all I knew, he wasn't there at all. I sat down on the ground and curled up into a ball. As the tears poured down my cheeks, I remembered how scared Gregory was of the dark.

All kids had their own irrational fears, but my son seemed to have some that were worse than what would be considered normal. The dark was an ongoing fear, even at his age. Pediatricians promised that he'd grow out of it by age five or so, but they didn't know my son. While he became overwhelmed by being over stimulated, under stimulation had a similar effect on his brain. He slept with a small nightlight by his bed, which gave him the perfect amount of vision, just in case he woke up in the middle of the night. He also played nature sounds on a little machine next to his head, soothing him to sleep every night. Being alone in the dark would be pure torture for my son.

Feeling angry and hopeless, I started sprinting through the maze, just so I could cover as much ground as possible. But with how worthless my flashlight was, I didn't see the brick wall around the corner until my face smashed into it.

I bolted upright, feeling wet spots on my face. But it was not blood. No, I had been sweating and crying in my sleep again. Feeling ill, I walked to the bathroom, hoping that I hadn't woken my mother. After splashing some cool water on my face, I sat on the toilet lid and held my head in my hands.

Just when I thought I was going to get some quality sleep, I was up before my alarm, willing myself not to throw up. There was never an escape from the madness. If I didn't have to imagine all of the horrible things that could be happening to my son during my waking hours, the nightmares wouldn't be so destructive. But my missing son and my attacker were always on my mind. Not even medication could fix that.

I couldn't do this anymore. I needed to find my son, but all of the information that I might have been able to share was locked away in my brain and I didn't have the access code to retrieve it. While I was afraid of what I had either lost completely or was purposefully blanking out, I still wanted information that would lead to my son. I was completely helpless.

At the same time, I couldn't help but feel as though I should be working so I could raise the funds needed to find a missing child. If things didn't go well, I would have to hire private investigators. Those were not cheap, and I didn't want to resort to begging others for the funds. However, with my mind constantly in other places, I don't know how I could focus for long enough to code. The focus I needed was just not there.

I could hear my mom's alarm clock going off. She'd traded her shift at work so she could visit my brother in the afternoon. I felt bad about not being able to make much of a financial contribution to the family. I had enough saved up for my son and me to live comfortably. I wasn't in a position where I could pay for a private investigator and pay for my brother's medical bills. If I could, I would have paid the difference that my mom would have lost, had she spent all of her time at the hospital. Unfortunately, I wouldn't be able to do any of those things unless I managed to create an app that sold really well.

Perhaps I would eventually find inspiration from the kidnapping to create something that would save lives. I already made an app that helps keep women safe after my abduction. Mine used GPS technology to send information to friends and family. When I was taken, nobody panicked immediately because I was supposed to be safe with my husband. So, when text messages and calls went unanswered by me, people just assumed that I was busy instead of being locked in a house with a rapist.

So, with my app, all a user has to do is add phone contacts to a special list. Then, if one of these people tries to contact the user and they don't respond within ten minutes, the contact receives the user's location on a map. It's not foolproof, but it protects a person's privacy while keeping their family in the loop.

Anyway, that was just one of my ideas that happened to catch on. Sometimes, app developers spend months working on something that never sells. I guess I happened to find a niche. It's unfortunate that I profit from people's insecurities, but at least I can justify it by knowing that it might save a life.

My other apps weren't as serious but still made decent money. One of the more successful ones was a game for kids with autism to practice coping skills in different stressful situations. Another one was just a way for new parents to track things like feedings and diaper changes. Now, with my son missing, I wondered if I would ever be able to successfully create an app to ensure that this never happened again.

I didn't want to speak with my mother, so instead of going downstairs for an early breakfast, I slipped back into bed. I had no intention of trying to fall back asleep, though. Instead, I checked my phone for missed messages, hoping to receive some more information from Detective Reyes. Unfortunately, there were only emails for twenty percent off children's clothes at a store that I frequent with Gregory. I kept it, in hopes that he could be home soon enough to use it.

Then, I went to the local newspaper's website, in hopes that there would be some sort of lead. But after scrolling through a few pages, I remembered that the police said they would not release too many details about the case, just in case it gave the kidnapper any information. I closed out of the browser and tossed my phone onto the other pillow.

The second the phone hit the satin case and slid under the covers, it began to vibrate. I scooted my hand underneath the sheet and lazily searched for it. I wasn't in the mood to talk to anyone, but on the off chance it was the police, I needed to answer it.

Jacob's name appeared on the screen and I thought about tossing it back onto the pillow. But for some reason, I kind of wanted to get this horrible dream off my chest, and I didn't have a therapy appointment scheduled for a few days. Reluctantly, I answered the phone and held it to my ear with a shaky hand.

"Hello?"

"Annabeth?" Jacob said in a breathy voice. "What are you doing up so early?"

"You're the one who called," I responded, a little confused by the tone of surprise.

"I guess you're right," he said, letting out a nervous laugh. "I couldn't sleep, and I was just thinking about yesterday. I hope you're not upset with me."

"No," I said sleepily. "I think we're all a little stressed out right now."

"Absolutely," he replied. "So, are you doing okay?"

My initial instinct was to lie, but there was so much I wanted to get off my chest, and Jacob was the only person available for listening.

"Actually, I'm not," I replied. "I had a really awful nightmare, and now I'm almost afraid to go back to sleep."

"What was it about?" he asked, sounding interested.

"I was looking for Gregory in the maze."

"The—the maze?" he stammered after a long pause.

"The maze that I was held captive in. I had a dream that Gregory was crying out for me, but I couldn't find him. I woke up before I could rescue him."

"Oh, Annabeth," he breathed. "Do you want to come over?"

I frowned. "Come over? It's early."

"Are you busy today?"

I scoffed. I knew I would do nothing but twiddle my thumbs all day and worry. "No, I don't have anything going on. I'm just waiting for an update."

"Come over for breakfast," he offered.

"Really?"

"Sure! I'll run down to the bakery and get those cheese Danishes you like. I can put on a pot of coffee too. How about you swing by in half an hour?"

"I don't know," I said hesitantly, staring down at my ragged pajamas.

"Come on," he said. "It'll be good for you. Don't you think you should get out of the house? I worry about your being all alone in there."

That fact hadn't crossed my mind until he mentioned it. He was right—I would feel a little safer being with someone else, even if it was just for an hour or so. By the time we were done, perhaps I could go back to the police station and check in.

"Yeah, okay," I replied. "I'm just going to get ready and then I'll head over."

"Awesome," Jacob replied, speaking a little faster. "See you soon."

I hung up the phone and stretched out in my bed. I heard my mom start her hair dryer, so I raced into the bathroom to take a quick shower before she left. I estimated that I had about three to five minutes to get out of the shower before she was gone. I hated the thought of standing naked under running water while home alone.

Of course, this was all just part of my daily routine. I had so many safeguards built into my schedule that these sorts of things didn't seem out of the ordinary for me. Occasionally, my therapist would give me a horrified look when I mentioned things like checking under the bed before I went to sleep and making fake phone calls when I was in public and felt nervous.

Unfortunately, my little rituals and habits weren't as effective as I might have hoped. Still, I clung to my routine as a mental safeguard, to at least give me the impression that I had an ounce of control over my life.

CHAPTER SIXTEEN

When I arrived at Jacob's small split-level house, I quickly ran to the front step while repeatedly hitting the lock button on my car's remote. The little beeps must have alerted Jacob to my arrival because he answered the door on the first knock.

"Hi," he wheezed. "Please, come in."

I followed him down the hall into his kitchen as his feet stomped on the hardwood floor. He had always been a big kid, but he had become quite rotund in the time since I had gone to school. I wondered if some of his unhealthy habits stemmed from his breakdown all those years ago. I had noticed that whenever I was feeling anxious, I ate poorly or ate nothing at all.

Jacob's house was nice, but bare. His bachelor pad

had no artwork or photographs adorning the walls. In fact, the only photo I could see was one of the two of us, standing in my front yard. I must have been in high school by then, and he was standing with a protective arm over my shoulder. I smiled when I saw the frame on his kitchen counter. He must have gotten it out to show me. The girl in the photo was so young and happy, completely oblivious to what life had in store for her.

"Have a seat," he said, gesturing to the table. I pulled out a chair and sat down, my feet tapping on the floor as I waited for him to join me.

I continued to look around the kitchen, trying to piece together my disjointed memories about my host. Did Jacob have other friends? Perhaps a girlfriend at some point? As I looked over the room, I saw dirty dishes in the sink and takeout packages stuffed in the trash. I didn't get the feeling that Jacob was used to having guests in his home. The kitchen didn't smell terrible, but it definitely didn't smell good. He was a loner.

"Here we go," he said with a smile on his face. He slid a stained mug in my direction, sloshing a few drops of steaming coffee down the side. Then, he opened the plastic clamshell container and dropped a pastry on each of our plates before licking the icing off his chubby fingers.

"Thanks," I said morosely. I pinched off an edge of the Danish and dropped it into my mouth. I had absolutely no appetite, but he had gone to the trouble to procure my favorite breakfast, so I obliged.

"So, why don't you tell me more about this crazy dream?" he said.

I nodded and started from the beginning, giving him details about how I felt in the maze. I described the cold brick walls, the soft earth beneath my feet, and the damp smell. He sat up a little straighter as I got into the details. I'm sure it sounded like the plot of a horror film to him.

"Wow," he said when I was finished.

"I know," I replied. "It's pretty messed up."

"It's absolutely fascinating," he said.

My stomach turned. I didn't find it fascinating as much as I found it horrifying. It was a poor choice of words on his part.

I fiddled with the hem of my shirt. I suddenly felt very uncomfortable and wanted to go home. Then, I remembered that it was still early in the morning and I would be alone. I should be thankful that someone was willing to sit beside me and listen.

Besides, I couldn't fault Jacob for what I thought was an inappropriate reaction to my fears. He was a bit of a social outcast. My son didn't always fit in with his peers, so I naturally felt drawn to those who could use a friend. If Jacob was being weird, it was only because he didn't know he was doing anything wrong. I needed to be more patient or I would lose him too.

"Is that really what it was like when you were held captive?" he asked.

I nodded. "Pretty much. It was always so dark and damp in there. I know it was a maze because I couldn't navigate around the space. But I have no idea what the layout was like."

"Do you remember where it was?"

I shook my head. "No. The therapist says it's possible that I'll never regain those memories."

"That's wild," he said. "What was it like in there? How did you feel?"

"In the dream?" I asked.

"No, in the maze."

I bit my lip. This was something I only really spoke to my therapist about.

"I don't need to burden you with this," I said dismissively. "I have a therapist for that. I can dump all of this stuff on her because she's a professional. You're not. You're just my friend."

"I can be more than your friend," he said. "I can be your confidant. Look, I think it's best to be able to speak about what's on our minds. I don't think you can talk to your family about this, can you?"

"No," I said mournfully. "I really can't. And you're right—sometimes, it's hard to keep this all to myself."

"Then tell me about it," he pried. "Come on, who am I going to tell?"

"I just don't quite understand why you want me to talk about it," I said. "It's really heavy stuff. Sometimes, I even feel like I'm going to force my therapist into therapy."

"She probably already is. Why don't you start with the maze? What's that like?"

I sighed. "Basically, just imagine a haunted house where it's dark and you don't know if something is going to pop out at you."

"I'm sure it's more complicated than that." he frowned. "I think you're smart enough to leave a haunted house."

"Well, not literally a haunted house," I replied, feeling frustrated. "It's unlike anything I've ever known. I tried so hard to find an exit, but it was just impossible. I remember a few little bits. There were two dead ends in a row. Then, there were a few curved areas that led back into the maze. I remember sleeping in one of those spaces because I could put my back up against the wall."

"That sounds scary."

"That's an understatement. There's no terror like it, except for maybe having my child taken from me. It was horrifying not knowing if I'd ever get out. Sometimes, I just wanted to die in there."

"Why?" he asked, his head tilted slightly.

"Because of how I was treated in there," I said, my voice cracking.

"What was the man like?" he pressed.

I shuddered. "Awful. Words don't even begin to describe how awful he is. He was big and often smelled bad. He covered my face when he had his way with me against my will."

"What?"

I let out a deep breath. "Yeah. That's exactly what it was. He pushed himself on me and made sure that I could never see his face very well. I kind of remember a time where I fought him off and removed the cover, but when I try to picture his face, it's just blank. I know it's not possible to have a completely blank face, devoid of all facial features, but that's what my memory came up with."

"Do you remember what his voice was like?"

"Not really," I admitted. "I know it was often angry. That's all I can remember."

"Really?" he said, an uncomfortable smile coming to his lips. "You've just blacked it out? You couldn't tell the cops what the guy looked or sounded like?"

"Nope," I replied. "Believe me, I wish it could. I've

been working with my therapist to draw it out of me. It's not easy, though."

"Don't you think that's dangerous?" he asked. "What if it's too much for your brain to handle? Maybe you lost those memories for a reason."

"It's a concern," I grumbled. "Still, I'll do anything to get my son back."

"Anything?"

"Anything."

I tried to eat another bite of the pastry, but it felt dry on my tongue. The cup of coffee sat steaming next to me, but I knew I couldn't stomach the acidic beverage. My appetite was already suppressed and my nerves were already jittery. The caffeine would make things far worse.

"What did it feel like when he did that to you?" he asked.

I frowned. I had never been asked that, not even by my therapist. Perhaps it was because I am a woman, but it seemed obvious. However, I didn't know if sexual assault carried the same weight in a man's eyes. Women were taught to fear it for as long as they understood it was a threat. Men didn't have to walk home at night with their keys in their fists, ready to strike or run if a man got too close. I knew it wasn't my job to teach him about it, but if I didn't educate him, who would?

"It's the worst thing a person could do to another," I said, trying to steady my voice. "It's used to show power over another. He didn't desire me—he just wanted to make me feel unsafe. And it worked. I lost the will to live. My husband was gone, and I thought I'd be subjected to that torture forever. I don't know how I made it out alive, but I did. Looking back, I'm glad I survived. I have a beautiful son and he means the world to me. But nothing scares me more than the prospect of him going through what I did."

"Maybe your captor does have feelings for you," he said. "Why else would he keep you to himself?"

I rolled my eyes. If this was Jacob being jealous of my rapist, I was not going to be happy. I dismissed the entire thought altogether. I knew that he didn't like my husband very much, but after what my mom told me about his protective nature, it kind of made sense. However, I would not sit and listen to him if he tried to tell me that he was jealous of the man who'd repeatedly had sex with me without my consent. Not a chance.

"I'm kind of tired," I said. "I might go home and try to rest."

"Is it something I said?" he asked.

"No," I lied. "I just didn't sleep well."

"Stay," he pleaded. "I'm worried about you. I don't think you should be alone right now. Why don't you sleep here until your mother gets home from work?"

I shook my head after entertaining the idea for a millisecond. I didn't really want to sleep—that would just invite more nightmares. I also didn't want to sleep in Jacob's bed. He would get too much satisfaction out of that.

"Fine, I'll stay for a little longer," I relented. "I just don't really want to talk about that part of my past, if that's okay."

"Sure," Jacob said, unperturbed. He took a big bite of his pastry, crumbs falling from his mouth. "So, are you sure that Gregory is being treated the same way you were?"

I shrugged. "I don't know. I have no way of knowing. If this monster can treat me like he has, then I think he can do the same with my son. The police are looking at all of the local pedophiles."

"What makes you think it was a pedophile?" Jacob asked, furrowing his brow.

"Who else steals a kid?" I asked.

He shrugged. "Someone who's obsessed with you. Maybe the guy just wants you and knows that your son is the easiest way to get to you. What do you think your attacker is doing to Gregory?"

"How should I know?"

"You know this guy better than anyone else. Think. Maybe it will help you find him."

"I try not to."

"It might help."

I winced as I tried to imagine my captor. He was big and had clammy hands. He slapped me around whenever I wouldn't comply. He was so rough with me.

"Gregory is difficult to deal with if you don't know what makes him tick. What scares me the most is that this man will harm him because he doesn't understand him. My son can lash out if he gets upset. I don't want him to get hurt because this man is frustrated with his behavior."

"I'm sure he's fine," Jacob said. "How did he hurt you?"

"He beat me," I said flatly.

"Yeah, but how did it feel?"

I glared at Jacob. I didn't like how he was using my horror story for his macabre interests. I understood that these types of accounts could be fascinating for some people. I just didn't think it was very tactful for my friend to ask me such personal questions.

"Do you know what I can tell you?" I asked, my eyes narrowing. Rage boiled under my skin. "I can tell you that if I ever discover who this sick freak is, I will personally kill him. I'll bash his brains in with a bat and slit his throat from ear to ear. I'll effing castrate him if I catch him."

This sudden outburst must have startled Jacob

because his coffee cup fell out of his hand and coffee splashed all over the table. I stood up quickly so it wouldn't run onto my lap.

"I'll get something to clean that up with," I said hurriedly, running to grab a towel. He wrenched it from my hands and swept up the liquid. After he wrung the towel into the sink, he sat back down, looking dismayed.

"I'm sorry if I startled you," I said sheepishly. "I just get so worked up about this stuff and never have the chance to let it out."

"It's fine," he said wearily. " I get it."

"Here, take my coffee," I said, pushing it toward his side of the table. "I don't think I can drink it anyway."

"No, it's yours," he insisted.

I took a few deep breaths, trying to calm down. I knew I shouldn't have taken my anger out on Jacob, but there was nothing I could do to help it. I was embarrassed by how I had acted around him.

"You don't mean that stuff," he said softly.

"Actually, I do," I said, my voice calmer now. "I didn't mean to startle you, but I stand by what I said. If I can hunt this guy down, I'll kill him."

"Don't," Jacob said, shaking his head. "You're only going to get yourself hurt. Now, drink your coffee and calm down."

My phone started buzzing, so I grabbed it from my

purse, relieved to have a distraction. After I read the messages, my jaw dropped open.

"What is it?" Jacob asked nervously. "Did they catch the guy?"

"No," I said, shaking my head. "My brother woke up. My mom's with him now. I have to go."

"Wait," he said, standing up from his chair. "You don't need to get yourself all worked up. I'm sure he's fine and you can talk to him later. Just stay here and finish your coffee."

"I'm sorry," I said, reaching for my car keys. "I have to go talk to him. He might have some information."

Before Jacob could get another word out, I was rushing out the door. I was so relieved that my brother had woken up and scared to hear what he had to say. But I knew that if he happened to see the attacker, he might be able to tell the police something useful.

As I sped down the street, I didn't even stop to check my surroundings. Usually, I made sure no one was hiding underneath my car or waiting for me around a corner. But this time, I was only aware of the fact that I needed to get to the hospital as quickly as possible. I didn't even notice Jacob standing on his front step with his hands on his hips as I drove away.

CHAPTER SEVENTEEN

Though I dreaded stepping foot back in that hospital, I burst through the door and strode up to the front desk. The smell of antiseptic made my skin crawl. It brought me back to my hospital room as I was being notified that my son was missing. My scalp was still bruised from my injury, and when I ran my hands through my hair, I could feel the spot where my skin was stapled back together. My skin was green underneath my eye as the broken blood vessels started to heal. I looked like hell, but I really didn't care.

"I'm here to see Tom Templeton," I said nervously. I clasped my hands together to stop them from shaking, but it was of no use.

"Ah, yes, you're his sister, correct?" the friendly

man behind the desk asked. He looked down the bridge of his nose through his bifocals as he typed on his computer.

"That's correct," I said meekly. I hoped he recognized me because my mom added me to the list of visitors, not because I was becoming a household name. While I didn't mind if people knew that there was a missing child to keep an eye out for, I didn't want to be pitied. My history of violent crimes committed against me was not what I wanted to be known for as a human being.

"Go through this door and to the left," he said as I was handed a visitor's name tag. "He is in Room 204. Your mother is in there now."

"Thank you so much," I said and rushed in the direction of Tom's room. My heart pounded as I walked and bile rose in my throat. I was afraid to face him.

When I got to the room, I saw my brother lying in his bed, looking broken. My mom sat by his side, her eyes wet with tears. I quietly opened the door and closed it behind me, slinking into the corner.

"Hi, Tom," I said softly, struggling to make eye contact with my older brother. "How are you feeling?"

He smiled. "Hey, Sis, I'm glad you're here."

I let out a shuddering sigh. My brother was too kind to me. He had always been a supportive big brother, always coming to my aid when I needed it. When I was brought home after being abducted, he took care of me. He was in nursing school at the time and spent his evenings off making sure that I was staying healthy. Being clueless about life when I was pregnant, he guided me through the process, always making sure I was feeling okay and talking through any symptoms or concerns I had. He even stepped in to be a male role model for Gregory since his father was not with us.

In my life, he had gone above and beyond to ensure that I was happy and healthy. And in return, I had allowed a stranger to enter his life and stab him in the back. He never needed to be part of my nightmare, yet anything I touched was certainly doomed. Because of this, I was racked with horrendous guilt. My family deserved better, yet I couldn't give that to them.

I picked up a chart on a side table and flipped through it. It was all medical terminology that flew right over my head. That's why I liked having my brother around. I could call him if Gregory had a cough or runny nose and he would tell me what to do. In return, any time he struggled with technology, I could set him straight. I had repaired a few hard drives that were on the brink of death and programmed apps into his phone. We worked well that way, always filling in each other's blind spot.

"How are you doing?" I asked sheepishly. Tom could hardly keep his eyes open, yet he smiled sleepily at me. I figured he was on a lot of drugs for the pain. I hated seeing him on his back. He was typically so active and lively. While I joked that he had replaced his sports team practices with snack cakes, he was still always on his feet, never stopping to rest.

"We're lucky he's awake," my mom answered for him. "He's also lucky he's not paralyzed. The doctor said that if the knife was just a millimeter closer to his spinal cord, he would never walk again."

"Really?" I breathed. I was glad that Tom was okay but sickened by the fact that it was possible that he would never walk again. He loved nursing, and I don't know what he would have done if he couldn't walk the halls of the hospital all day.

"Yep," she said coldly. "He's going to have to go through a lot of physical therapy. It could be over a month before he's back at work. Even then, he's going to have to take it easy. I just hope he's able to keep his job."

"I'm sure he'll be able to," I said, though not entirely sure. "He's good at his job. They need him."

"Well, he's got a long road to recovery," she said, stretching her legs in front of her. "Besides the stabbing, he's got a fractured wrist from the accident. It's just a hairline fracture, so he'll get the cast off before he's done with therapy. He's got a lot of swelling in his spine, so he's on a ton of medication. He has to be sedated so he can stay still and not cause any more damage. The surgeons here are excellent. Things could have been a lot worse."

"It's fine," Tom said. "I'm okay. I'm glad Annabeth is okay. I heard that you hit your head."

"Yeah," I replied casually. "I had a concussion and a few staples in my head."

"Ouch," he replied. "Feeling okay? Any memory loss?"

"Yep," I said flatly. "How about you?"

"Same here," he slurred. "Mom told me everything she knew. She said we were decorating the Christmas tree when we had a break-in and I got stabbed. Then, Gregory . . ."

His voice trailed off. My lip quivered when I saw how sad he looked.

"Do you know anything about where he might be?"

I shook my head. "I hoped you might know something."

"I wish I did. I hope he's found. I bet you're so scared."

"I am," I said softly. "The police are working very hard."

"Good. There are some good men and women there. They'll find him."

My mom stood up and looked over at Tom. His eyelids were drooping and a thin stream of drool fell onto his pillow.

"It's the medication," she explained. "We should let him rest. His body has undergone extreme trauma and sleep is vital to his recovery."

"I hoped he'd remember the attacker."

"Maybe he'll remember when he's had some rest. You don't need to bother him while he's recovering. If he remembers anything, I'm sure he'll tell you."

As we walked out of his room, I looked back at my older brother. He was now sleeping peacefully as the monitor near his bed beeped in a steady rhythm.

"Leave him alone," my mom said. "He's been though enough. This wasn't his problem to begin with."

I bit my tongue so hard that it nearly bled as she marched me out of the hospital. She pulled me into her car, even though mine sat on the other side of the lot.

"Get in," she ordered.

"But mine—"

"Just do as I say. We need to talk."

"You're right about that," I retorted. I was becoming increasingly agitated by my mother's hostility toward me.

Once the doors were closed and our seatbelts were buckled, she turned toward me, pursed her lips, then turned back toward the steering wheel and started the car.

"What do you want to say?" I asked as she cruised out of the parking lot.

"I don't know. I'm just very worried about your brother."

"So am I," I replied, furrowing my brow. "And I'm worried about my son. In fact, that crazy psycho can swoop in and take me at any moment, but that's really the least of my concerns at the moment. Actually, I'd say I'm least concerned about the fact that my mother is being very passive-aggressive toward me and I don't even know what I did."

"Tom had nothing to do with this. I'm horribly sorry about your husband and your son. Hell, I'm still messed up about what you went through. But I don't know why the whole family is being involved. Your brother is so innocent. Now, who knows if he'll ever return to his former self? He had a bright future ahead of him. He was starting to make some good money. He'd been on dates with some very promising women. You didn't know this because you were wrapped up in your own world, but he was getting serious with one."

"I didn't know that."

"Of course, you didn't," she snapped. "You were being a paranoid mess. Your son spent so much time at his tutor's house that he'd accidentally call me by her name. The whole thing just makes me sick. As a mother and a grandmother, I can't let everyone I care about get hurt. Am I going to be next? Is this sick freak going to come after me because I'm your mother? Why can't he just . . ."

Her voice trailed off as she realized she was yelling at her daughter. I sat with a stony expression, not giving her the satisfaction of getting to me.

"Why can't he just take me? I've wondered the same thing. You don't have to try too hard to make me feel bad. I already feel terrible about what happened to Tom. I'm obviously distraught that my son is missing. I would be devastated if anything happened to you. You can't make me feel worse than I already do. I can't go much lower. Is this what you want to do? Did you want to berate me for having a stalker that I can't shake?"

My mom sighed dramatically and took the next corner a little too fast for my liking. Fortunately, if we got pulled over, any cop in the area would recognize us. I was becoming the town's freak show.

"You've got to know something, Annabeth. How could you acquire a stalker? Who have you met that could take an interest in you and go so far as to harm your family? Was there someone in college who was pissed at Greg? Did you go on any dates before him?"

"No!" I answered loudly. "I mean, I don't

remember anyone. Maybe there was someone and I'm just blacking out his face."

"That's just too convenient," she groaned. "You've experienced so much, yet you can't give any helpful information."

"I'm trying," I cried. "I really am."

"Yeah, I know," she said harshly. "I just wish you'd try a little harder. There's so much at stake here. The police need information from you. Everyone knows you have it, but you're not allowing yourself to release it."

"Take that up with my therapist, won't you? In the meantime, do you want me to move out so I won't endanger you?"

My mother looked like I'd slapped her across the face. "Absolutely not. You know how much money I spent on home security features to keep everyone safe? That house is the best place for you to be, and I won't hear of your leaving because of some disagreement. I'm frustrated as heck, but you're still my daughter. I have a responsibility to keep you safe, even though the other people I love are getting hurt in the meantime."

Tears streamed down my cheeks. I felt terrible about what had happened in the last attack, but there was nothing I could do. Her anger felt misguided.

"I am not the attacker," I said firmly. "If you want to be mad at that freak, be my guest. He's the one who killed Greg. He's the one who injured Tom and kidnapped Gregory. He's the one who brutally attacked and violated and had his way with me. He did this to us. I may not remember everything, but I'm fairly confident that I never did anything to deserve this. Now, do you really think that I deserve all the blame for what happened to Tom?"

"No, but—"

"But what?" I interrupted.

"But we don't know who it is," she said, her voice tired.

"What difference does that make?" I asked.

"Maybe we should have tried harder after Greg was killed," she said.

"There were homicide detectives on that case," I pointed out.

"I still feel like we gave up too easily," she said.

"Maybe that was because I had a baby on the way and I was mourning the loss of my husband. Then, once I had Gregory, I was in over my head. He had special needs, but I was still his primary caregiver. I had help, of course, but it was so hard to work while trying to soothe my inconsolable son. I'm sorry if I didn't have the time or the money to hire people to find the guy who did this to our family. That was some time ago. There have been more advances in technology since then."

"I've told the nurses to look out for a strange man coming to visit Tom," my mother said. "They have cameras in that building. If anyone comes through to finish the job, we'll know."

I bit my tongue again. While it was troubling that someone attacked Tom, I knew that the assailant was really after me. I highly doubted he wanted to kill Tom. If anything, he just wanted to get Tom out of the way because he was protecting me. My mom was a short woman with little athletic ability. If someone came after me, she would not be capable of doing much. Tom, on the other hand, was fairly big. At the very least, he was an imposing presence. But I didn't want to explain this to my mom. She was too busy worrying about her precious son to realize that my life was in peril. In the last few weeks, I had been thinking about what my stalker would do if he got his hands on me. Because he tried to keep me and failed, the next step would be to keep me forever—in a way that I would never be able to escape. I think he planned to kill me.

When we pulled up in the driveway, I noticed that there was a large package stuffed in the mailbox. I looked over at my mother, who had also noticed it.

"What did you order?" I asked.

She shook her head. "Whatever it is, I don't think it's for me. Besides, it's way too early for the mail to be here. It never arrives until after two."

Frowning, I jumped out of the car and strode over to the mailbox. There, on the center of the white bag was my name, written in thick, black block letters. My heart sank. It had to have been from him.

There was no address or postage on the package, so it couldn't have been sent through the mail. Someone had waited until the house was empty and placed it there, knowing that I would see it as soon as I got home. The lettering on the bag was so unnatural that it couldn't possibly be traced back to anyone through standard handwriting analysis.

"I don't want anything to do with that," my mom said, real fear in her voice. She hurried inside the house and began to set the alarms. I noticed that she had added a small canister of pepper spray to her keychain. Looking up and down the street, I couldn't see anything out of the ordinary, so I grabbed the package and ran up the steps, locking the front door behind me. Logically, I knew that it was stupid to take a strange package into my house, but my instinct told me that I needed to open it for answers. I didn't care if there was a message laced in Anthrax—I just needed the message to find my son.

CHAPTER EIGHTEEN

By now, my mom had holed herself up in her bedroom, likely with a surgical mask on her face and a blast shield near her body. Having faced death myself, I didn't have the same protective measures in place at the moment. I certainly didn't want to be annihilated by this freak, but more importantly, I didn't want my son to fall victim for any longer. If I were meant to play a game, I would play to win.

I set the white package in the center of the kitchen table. In a moment of clarity, I found a pair of dishwashing gloves under the sink and slipped them on. If there was something dangerous inside, I didn't need it all over my skin. Then, holding my breath, I carefully cut the top of the wrapping off. Just in case, I took a few steps back, only to see a photo slip out of the plastic.

My heart was pounding as I approached the table. I flipped the picture over in my hand and realized that it came from an old Polaroid camera. I hadn't seen one of those used in years. I squinted my eyes to make out what was in the photo. It was dark, save for a blurry shape in the center.

I felt incredibly dizzy. My vision narrowed to a tiny dot in the center of my eyes, so I sat down on a chair and dropped my head to my knees. I clamped my mouth shut so I wouldn't vomit as a wave of memories came back to me. They were disjointed, like little flashes of light in front of me. It was as if I was watching an old slide projector run out of order. I saw my attacker's feet coming toward me, then I saw the brick wall in front of my face.

"Mom," I moaned as loudly as I could. I don't think she heard me. It wouldn't surprise me at this point if she didn't want anything to do with me. I was the cause of her misery. I didn't want to be a burden, but if I passed out, I wanted someone around. I didn't want her to walk in on me sprawled out on the floor. She would immediately suspect the worst, and not the fact that my tormenter knew exactly how to play me.

I was still wheezing between my knees when I heard tentative footsteps coming down the hall.

"What is it?" she asked, half-scared, half-annoyed.

"Just pictures," I whimpered. "It's just photos."

"Of what?" she asked, her voice lowering an octave.

I held out the photo without looking at it. She studied it for a moment, her brow sinking as she tried to make sense of it.

"I don't understand," she said. "It's blurry. I can't make out what it's supposed to be. Are you sure it wasn't coated in something? Do I need to call an ambulance?"

I shook my head violently. "No, Mom, it's the maze. I would recognize it anywhere. It's hard to see because the light wasn't on. That's the maze he kept me in. He's trying to tell me something."

Her eyes widened as she understood what I was saying. She sat beside me at the table, her hands folded in front of her.

"What are the other photos of?" she asked slowly. "Annabeth, are they just photos of the maze, or is there something more?"

I shrugged as I finally rose up to face her. "I don't know. I just saw the maze and I thought I was going to faint. I'm afraid to look at the others."

"I know," she said, finally sounding supportive. "I'm right here. I think you need to look at the others."

"Okay," I said, beginning to remove my gloves. I

figured that the psychological threat was the only intent.

"Keep those on," she ordered. "You're dealing with evidence."

"Right," I said. "Should we call the police?"

"I'll call Detective Reyes right now," she said, scurrying out of the room.

I took a deep breath and pulled the gloves up a little tighter. I needed to be able to keep it together for just a few more minutes. My son depended on me.

I scooped the remaining photos out of the bag and began to flip through them like a deck of cards. There had to have been around thirty of them stacked in my hand.

The next few in line were just other parts of the maze in the dark. These, I remembered quite vividly because I spent so much time crawling along the floor with my hands against the wall. With each blurry shot, I remembered how I rubbed my fingertips raw on the grout as I searched for an exit. In time, it was almost as though I was flipping through an old yearbook as I remembered horrible times in my life.

The next one was different. Here, the lights in the maze were on. I didn't remember there being overhead lighting. My memories mostly circled around the dark, or in a few instances, dim light that illuminated my captor. This view of the maze in harsh, fluorescent lighting was one that I had never seen before. It looked like a crime scene photo, though I knew that only one man held the secrets of his lair.

"I talked to the detective," my mom said, rushing back into the kitchen. "He'll be here soon. What have you found?"

"There are lights," I said stupidly. "I don't remember there being lights in the maze. I never saw his face. If there were lights, I'm sure I would have seen them eventually."

"He probably didn't turn them on often. It would be too easy to find a way out."

"I guess," I said, not entirely convinced that she was right. It was easier to blame a faulty memory.

I flipped to the next picture and screamed. In one of the rounded sections of the maze where I frequently slept, was my son. He had his little arms tied behind his back, a cloth gag around his face, and a rope around his ankles. My mom looked over my shoulder and sharply inhaled, sucking the breath between her teeth.

I studied the picture, trying to examine my son through a tiny piece of film. He looked sleepy and I feared that he had been drugged so he would cooperate. I wondered if I was drugged and if that was why so many of my memories were gone. He didn't look scared, necessarily, but he also didn't look like he was in his right mind. If my son knew he was in trouble, he would be hell to deal with. My guess was that he'd tried to escape and got too close for his own good.

His shirt was stretched out and his shoes were missing. The bottoms of his white socks were stained brown from the dirty maze. I hoped he wasn't too cold. The picture was blurry, so I couldn't tell if he had bruises on his body or if I was just seeing shadows. I was relieved that there was a picture of him at all, clearly alive and relatively untouched.

The next picture was the same shot, but from a different angle. Here, I could see his arms behind his back. His wrists looked raw and red where the bindings pressed into his skin. I grimaced as I thought about how my baby was processing the pain. He spent most of his time inside and away from anything that could cause him physical pain, so I wasn't sure how he handled the pain of being tied up and pushed around. It wasn't as if he had gotten a taste of rough behavior from organized sports.

"My baby," I wailed. My mom's face turned white. She had helped raise her only grandchild. Now, with so much uncertainty in her children's' future, she feared she'd never have another chance at being a grandmother.

My mother was very good with Gregory. While it seemed as though she was tired of my relying so heavily on others, she never treated him like it was a chore to watch him. She was amazed at his intelligence and stuck every aced test to the refrigerator. She bought him expensive building sets and complex books to keep his mind busy. From the time he could speak, she always bragged to her coworkers about how she had the next Albert Einstein at home.

"He looks okay," she said softly, trying to get me to calm down. "Don't you think he looks okay?"

I looked at the picture again. He certainly wasn't okay, but I knew what she meant.

"He's not dead," I replied. "He's still alive. We still have time."

"That's right," my mom said as I continued on through the pictures. In the next one, his eyes were wide with fear and his mouth was open. I could practically hear him crying out in that one.

"Jeez," my mom hissed. "Who does this to a child? He's the most innocent kid I know."

"Someone who wants to get to me," I replied. "I have to say, it's working. If he's trying to lure me to him, I think he's got me figured out. I'd break down those brick walls for him."

The next couple of pictures were more of the same. In each one, Gregory looked either scared or sleepy, possibly depending on the effect of the drugs at the time. Then, there was one with the lights off and a dim beam of light shining on my son's face.

"Oh, it's dark," I said, my voice quivering. "He must have screamed for the guy to turn the lights on. I know my son—if it was too dark and he was scared, he wouldn't stop screaming until they came on."

"Maybe that's why he was gagged," my mom suggested. "This guy doesn't know who he's dealing with. Of course the poor kid is going to scream and cry. I would do the same, and I'm an adult."

Much to my shock, the next photos weren't of my son at all, but of me. I almost didn't recognize myself at first, but as I stared at my body in the light, I was able to put myself back into the maze.

I wasn't even aware that my mom was looking at the picture until she gasped. I dropped the stack to the table and covered it with my hands. I felt violated all over again. My privacy had already been taken from me when he'd stripped me naked and had his way with me, then again when I was examined by a doctor and interrogated by police. Now, there was evidence that I had been violated, and now, people would have to see it.

"Do you want me to look for you?" my mom asked.

"No," I said before quickly flipping through the pictures of me. None were all too explicit, but several featured me in various stages of undress, pleading for him to stop. I didn't even realize at the time that I was being documented in such a way. Add that to the list of things I didn't remember.

I saw the marks on my body, the ones he'd made when I tried to fight him off. I had spent months rubbing special ointment into those scars to fade them to the point where they weren't obvious. In my mind, if I eliminated the physical scars, the psychological ones would disappear along with them.

I was also struck by how young I looked in the photo. While I was still relatively thin, I looked skinny like a child in the photo. I looked like a teen, because I was one. I was in college at the time, and still incredibly naïve. I would give anything to have that innocence again. Most girls learned the ways of the world bit by bit. If they were lucky, their education would be through anecdotes from others and seemingly benign personal experiences. I learned how quickly things could go bad in a span of a few days.

I remembered my long hair that I had grown out for my wedding. I continued to grow it for our honeymoon because Greg once mentioned how much he liked it long. I cut it to my chin after he died. I didn't feel like the same woman anymore, and I needed a look to match how I saw myself. That, and it was easier to keep my scalp lacerations clean with short hair.

I noticed that in one of the photos, my wedding ring was missing. I twirled it around my finger as I looked at the photo. If he took it from me, I don't know how I got it back. I figured that would be a prime opportunity to take a token from me. Whatever happened, I was grateful that it was back on my finger.

The last photos were of Gregory again. In one, the lights were on and he was facing a wall. In another, a lantern was illuminating the space. Apparently, he had managed to fall asleep in a ball on the ground. Then in another, he was staring down at the ground, a look of rage on his face. I understood where he was coming from. I was angry too.

When I reached the end of the stack, I started over from the beginning, poring over all of the small details that had been overshadowed by the big picture. Once I looked beyond my son and me in the center of many of the photos, I noticed things that I hadn't realized when I was within the maze.

When I compared the pictures of my son and me, I noticed that the construction had aged considerably. In the ten-year span, the wooden beams had changed color with the air. In my son's photos, cobwebs clouded the corners. A few times, I was able to match specific locations in both sets of photos. As far as I could tell, he was in the exact same hell I'd lived through, just ten years apart. I wondered if anyone else had been stuck down there in the meantime, or if it was a creation just for my own displeasure. While I hoped that no one else had to be subjected to that torture, it seemed so extreme that someone would build such a labyrinth to torment one person.

So, that ruled out the possibility of a second location and a copycat. If was safe to say that my stalker had been near for quite some time. I couldn't remember anything about the location of the maze, but if it was in the vicinity of the stalker's house, it could be useful to the police. With any luck, my son was near. It was now just a matter of finding him.

I now felt a particular sense of kinship with my young son. Though I never wanted him to go through any of the nightmares I'd experienced in my young life, at least I would know what he was going through. I didn't want to have this connection with him, but we really had no choice.

My mom returned to the table with two steaming cups of lemon and ginger tea. I took a small sip, letting the hot liquid settle my stomach. She set out a plate of cookies beside the white bag, but I wasn't interested in eating right now. Instead, I went into detective mode, trying to find meaning in the photos. I wasn't entirely sure why my stalker was sending these pictures to me in the first place. Did he want to show me that he could easily rattle me with a small package? Or did he want to communicate the fact that my son was still alive and relatively untouched? It seemed particularly cruel to include pictures of me, though, which led me to believe that the guy was messing with me.

I wasn't a psychologist by any means. I'd spent the last ten years wondering what a stranger would want to do with me. I thought back to what my mom had said about encountering someone in my past and paying no mind. I feared that there was some guy in a college class that I'd inadvertently slighted by ignoring him. I was very studious in the early days of college, so if a guy tried to ask me out during class or something, I may have refused because I didn't know what was going on. Besides, I had been with Greg for awhile, so I had a built-in excuse. Other than that, I couldn't think of a single man in this world who had something against me or a reason to become infatuated with me. Nothing came to mind.

"For the detective," my mom said as she slid a plate of scones onto the table. She bumped the white plastic envelope, sending it floating onto the floor. I scowled at her as she prepared her home for our guest. I was far more concerned with the status of my child than whether the detective was well-fed. I didn't have a problem with Detective Reyes, but we didn't need to impress him for any reason. He worked for us, and I doubted that a leftover scone or some oatmeal raisin cookies would produce better results. He wanted to find my son as much as we did. I scooted my chair away from the table and grasped at the object that had fallen to the ground.

When I picked it up, I realized that I had not completely emptied it of its contents. A tiny sliver of computer paper stuck to the inside of the plastic, like a fortune in a takeout cookie. I pulled it out and read its message, typed in a bold, black font.

Come be a family with us.

I tossed it onto the table, watching it flutter onto the stack of photos. "Over my dead body," I growled.

CHAPTER NINETEEN

I didn't even notice that my mom had let Gabriel inside. I was too busy sitting at the table, absolutely fuming at my stalker and his message to me. I didn't have the patience for games.

"Annabeth," the detective said, rushing in. "Are you okay? Your mom said you received something in the mail. She believed that it was from your stalker."

"Yeah, it's him," I said flatly. "He even gave me the courtesy of writing a note."

Detective Reyes's eyes popped open.

"It was typed," I said, sliding it across the table. "You won't get a handwriting analysis from that. The package has writing on it, but I doubt it's useful."

The detective studied the note, then looked to the package. He pursed his lips the whole time.

"Am I right?" I asked.

"Most likely," he said quickly. "We'll compare it to some other samples back at the precinct."

"Any leads?" I asked as I twiddled my thumbs.

He shook his head. "Actually, yeah, I do," he said after thinking for a moment. "After we last spoke, Morrie Jenkins died by suicide."

I raised my eyebrows. "Do you think it's because he had something to do with it?" I started breathing faster until I felt like I had sucked all the oxygen in the room.

"No idea." He frowned. "We're still working on it. It makes things a little harder if he's dead. But, there's a good chance he wasn't your stalker—not directly, anyway."

"How do you know?" I asked, my face feeling flushed.

"Well, do you remember when we were chased by that guy in the mask?"

"Yeah, I remember it well," I said dryly.

"Well, that wasn't Morrie. He was still in the interrogation room being questioned when we were chased. It wasn't him. It could be an accomplice or a hired hand, but it wasn't Morrie."

I hung my head. I didn't want Morrie to be my attacker because I didn't want a pedophile anywhere near my son. But I didn't like the idea that my captor was still at large. Now, a man was dead because of my accusations. I mean, he wasn't a good man by any regards. And if he killed himself after dealing with the police, then it was likely that he had something to hide. Still, I didn't feel good about having a dead guy involved with my investigation.

"I know, it's hard to hear. He was a pedophile and we have some people investigating him still. We're pretty wary about him. He was an old guy, and prison hadn't reformed him whatsoever. If he hadn't already broken the law, he was waiting for an opportunity. He's not a loss to society. It's still not pleasant, though."

"Yeah, I get that," I said. "Well, at least your list of suspects is down by one."

"Not sure if that helps," he admitted. "So, can you show me what the bastard sent you? I'm glad you thought to put on gloves. We'll definitely have these checked for prints. Now, if you don't mind, I'd like for you to explain these photos to me as best as you can. You're in a unique position because you've seen this place before. My job is to provide an outside perspective and catch things you were too close to see. How does that sound?"

"Fine," I said warily. "I guess we'll start here," I said, showing him the pictures of the room.

"This is the maze?" he asked.

"The one and only. I actually remember some of these parts."

I held the pictures in front of his face, trying my best to keep my hands from shaking so he could get a good look. Eventually, I decided it was best to slide them across the table and have him lean down for a closer look.

"I'm sure you've read the old reports, but I don't recall finding an exit to this place. I mean, obviously, I got out, but I don't know how. I do remember frantically searching, though."

"Yeah, I remember that," he said distractedly as he looked through the photos of the brick labyrinth. "Someone spent a lot of time on this."

"He included my son in these ones," I said, passing over the next set. "He's missing some clothing, but it doesn't look like he was hurt too badly. My son would have made a big ruckus if he was uncomfortable, so I'm not surprised this guy couldn't handle the noise."

"I'm so sorry," he breathed. He stared at the photos, the wheels in his brain spinning furiously.

"I guess I should be thankful that he's alive," I said. "That's what's most important right now."

"This is true," Gabriel muttered. "I'm shocked by how many photos the guy sent of Gregory. I've been trying to work on a profile for this guy, and these photos help a lot."

Next, I passed the photos that I was featured in. For a split second, I thought about hiding them under the envelope or throwing them away. I didn't want to withhold evidence because it could potentially help our case, but I really didn't want Detective Reyes to see me like this.

I knew that he had already seen the photos that the police took when I filed my initial report ten years ago. Because of the locations of my injuries, I was mostly undressed for those shots. This was different. When he looked at the pictures from my file, I wasn't sitting beside him, explaining what had happened to me. Now, I had to look at him as he examined my naked body at the most vulnerable point in my life. It was absolutely embarrassing.

But there was no way I could hide the photos. If it helped him figure out who took Gregory, then it would be worth it. In the meantime, I just had to suck it up and allow for my body to be on display.

Thankfully, the detective was highly professional and sensitive to my embarrassment. He quickly looked at the photos as I muttered an explanation about what he was seeing. He nodded his head and added the photos to the stack.

My face was burning by now. I got up and walked to the kitchen sink as he flipped through the stack of photos. I grabbed a glass from the cupboard and filled it with cold water, drinking it slowly to buy myself a little more time before I had to sit beside Gabriel. I turned back to watch him bite his bottom lip as he tried to find meaning in the package. My stomach fluttered for some reason, so I chugged the rest of the water and walked around the kitchen in an attempt to settle my nerves.

"What's the verdict?" my mom asked nervously, nibbling on the side of the scone that she'd set out for the detective.

"I've been formulating a profile," he said slowly. "I'm glad this guy sent you the photos. It helps a lot."

"Does it?" I asked.

"I think so. I think we're definitely looking at a psychopath."

"Why do you think that?"

"Well, for starters, it doesn't seem as though he has empathy. He's supposed to be obsessed with you, yet he does things to hurt you. And because it appears you don't have any known enemies, I'd say that he's infatuated with you. He's in love with you but doesn't care if you're hurt in the process. That's abnormal for your average human. When you're in love with someone, you're supposed to do whatever you can to protect them from harm."

My face reddened a little deeper. The thought of someone loving me in the way I wanted to be loved made me break out in a sweat. The way Gabriel described it was just too tender and pure. It made me nauseated.

"The psychopath is often very intelligent and can fit into society without causing alarm bells to go off. Usually, these people rise to the top of their field—we're talking CEOs and business owners. Part of their success comes from not having to worry about screwing other people in the process to get to the top."

"You think that my stalker is a CEO?" I asked, perplexed that anyone with real power would want something to do with me.

"Not necessarily. That's just a common example. These people are also somewhat likely to play games with their victims because they think they're too smart to get caught. In this case, it's been really hard to track this person down, in part to your amnesia. He's trying to play a game with you by taking your son and delivering these bad memories. He's a cocky son of a bitch. He's been careful to not include anything that can identify him. But, with any luck, that hubris will lead to his demise. He may be smart, but we're just as clever."

I felt a small wave of relief wash over me. It really seemed like Detective Reyes knew what he was talking about.

"So, I think it's pretty safe to say that this guy is fairly smart. After all, he's built a maze and has managed to go undetected for this long. We're probably looking at someone who can keep up a fairly normal life."

I shook my head. "There's nothing normal about this guy. He's truly awful."

"I don't disagree. Would you say that he has emotional instability?"

"I've only experienced unstable behavior, so yes."

"So, we can maybe assume that he's been ticketed for minor crimes. Maybe he's gotten speeding tickets or warnings for erratic driving. But, I don't necessarily think we're looking at a felon. He's a planner and well-organized. Criminals who have been through the system are usually dumb and get caught easily. But since he's managed to evade us for this long, I'm confident that he's no dummy."

"That's not encouraging."

He gave me a reassuring smile. "No, he'll slip up eventually. They eventually do. I'm also going to look into people who have a background in handiwork. It's possible that this guy had someone do the maze construction for him. If so, it would be too easy for us to get someone to crack. If he did the work himself, then that should help us narrow things down. My guess is that a guy like this is proud of his handiwork. Does anyone like this come to mind?"

"Not really," I muttered.

"That's okay. We can figure this out. The thing I don't understand is, why didn't he take you instead of your son? Your brother was disabled and your son is too little to stop someone capable of kidnapping. He could have snatched you out of the shower instead of taking your son. It seems foolish for a smart man to increase his chances of getting caught if he's really just after you."

I swallowed hard. "I think it's the game. It's like he gets off on this stuff. In his note, he mentioned being a family. I'm really worried that he's not going to let go of Gregory."

Gabriel's face fell. "I think you might be right. He's potentially not using Gregory as leverage. He's trying to complete the whole set. He got your husband out of the way. Now, he's got your only child. In the end, he'll try to take you so he can create his own family. This is someone who either doesn't have a family of his own or who spends enough time away from them that he could pull this off. He's trying to replace your husband. He could hold you two underground for life."

I felt like the air had been knocked out of my lungs. Everything Gabriel said made perfect sense. It was strange that as someone who had been repeatedly assaulted by this monster, I didn't know him as well as a police officer who was new to the case. If anything, I should have been an expert on the guy, not Gabriel.

After much insistence on my mom's part, Gabriel took a cookie and a cup of coffee. He was careful not to eat and drink too close to the photos, lest he contaminate the evidence. He engaged in some small talk with my mother, though I tuned it out. I really didn't care about hospital security, nor did it seem pertinent to the case. After hearing Detective Reyes's description of my stalker, it didn't seem as though Tom was in any more danger. I doubted that my brother fit into his ideal family fantasy.

"I'm going to have to take the package with me," the detective said, jolting me from my daydream in which I killed my stalker.

"Oh, yeah, sure," I muttered. I had no use for it, nor did I want pictures of my terrified son in my house. I knew that if I had them in my possession, I would be tempted to look at them. I preferred to have them destroyed, but the police could utilize them better than I could anyway.

"Unless there's anything else you need me for, I think I'll take these to the lab and have them processed into evidence. I'll let you know if we find any fingerprints or DNA. It's probably not likely, but we'll give it a close look anyway."

"Thanks," I said weakly. "I appreciate your help."

"No problem," he said. "What do you have planned for the rest of your day?"

I couldn't come up with a response. I stood there with my mouth open, somehow stunned by the fact that he was asking me if I had plans.

"I—I don't know," I stuttered.

"I only ask because you clearly have someone after you," he replied calmly. "If I have a general idea of what you plan on doing, I'll be the first one there if anything goes wrong."

"Oh," I said, my face falling. "I hadn't really thought about that yet. My mind has been all over the place."

"I didn't mean to bother you," he said quickly, looking sheepish. "I promise I'm not trying to invade your privacy. You really don't have to tell me. This isn't part of my official questioning."

"Oh, no, it's fine," I said, understanding what he was after. "Like I said, I haven't really planned out my day. I might be back at the hospital to see my brother at some point. Is there anything I should or shouldn't be doing?"

He nodded. "If you're going out alone, maybe tell your mother your plans."

I hid my scoff. I wasn't particularly pleased with my mother at the moment. Of course he would tell me to give my mom my location. It was just like being a teen again.

"Maybe try to relax and see if any memories come

back to you," he suggested. "I don't want to put any pressure on you, but we could really use a lead."

I nodded. "Maybe I can get in to see my therapist. I tend to remember more after we talk."

"That would be awesome," he said, his voice full of excitement. Suddenly, I felt like I had no choice but to go. I really wanted to find my son, and for some odd reason, felt the need to impress the detective. If I could help him do his job in the process of getting my life back to normal, then I would be happy.

"Well, keep me updated," he said. "Good luck with your therapist, and make sure to call 911 if you think you might be in danger. Even if it's just a funny feeling in your gut, it's better to be safe than sorry."

"Got it," I replied. "Thanks for coming by."

"Anytime," he said, flashing me a smile. He gathered up the evidence and put it into a plastic bag, zipping up the top. I sank back down into my chair as he said goodbye to my mother and let himself out of the house. I couldn't quite explain the feeling, but I really didn't want him to go.

CHAPTER TWENTY

After a few hours of sitting at the kitchen table, staring at the wall, I got a call back from my therapist. Her receptionist must have heard the desperation in my voice because I wasn't expecting to get into her office on such short notice. When I heard Dr. Andrews on the line, nervous excitement flooded my body. With any luck, talking to her would help me make sense of the pictures and potentially help out with the case.

"James gave me your message," the therapist said. "I understand that there was a recent development in your case that you need to discuss."

"That's right," I said breathlessly. "I don't want to talk about it over the phone in case anyone is listening."

"Of course," she replied calmly. "Do you think you could come in at two?"

"Yes, that works," I said eagerly.

"Excellent. I'll have you added to the schedule. Do you think you're ready for more intense hypnotherapy?"

I bit my lip. I was scared that it wouldn't work and terrified that it would. "I don't know. I want to remember, but—"

"I understand," she replied. "I have to go to an appointment now, but we can discuss our options more when you get here. I look forward to seeing you soon."

"Thanks," I said meekly before hanging up the phone.

My mom walked into the kitchen and slipped her shoes on at the door. "Who was that?" she asked.

"Therapist," I responded flatly. "I suppose I'm supposed to tell you that I'm going to see her in a little bit. Do you want to tell me where you're going, or is this just a one-way street kind of thing?"

She raised an eyebrow at me. "If you must know, I'm going to cover part of a shift. My schedule has been so messed up recently, and others have been helpful in covering for me, so I don't really have a say when I work. I have an appointment with my own therapist, and then I'm going to see your brother."

"Really?" I asked.

"This is all very stressful," she replied hastily. "I prefer to talk to someone who can provide me with good advice, rather than load myself up on booze every night. It's still new to me, so I don't really want to talk about it. I'll be home later."

"Okay," I said softly. When she closed the door behind her and the alarm reset, tears welled up in my eyes. I was ruining everyone's lives. That was another thing I had to bring up to my therapist.

At a quarter till two, I stuffed a folder and my anti-anxiety medication into my purse and marched out the door, trying to feign confidence. I purposefully looked both ways down the street before getting into my car. Then, I quickly locked the doors and started the engine.

When I got to the office, I took a few minutes to practice breathing deeply. I wanted to show Gloria that her brilliant work was helping me, even though I felt like a wreck. I got out of my car and jogged to the door, making eye contact with the camera attached to the front of the building. I always parked as close to security cameras as possible.

In the waiting room, the receptionist handed me a cup of herbal tea. I took a small sip and watched small particles float to the bottom of the cup.

"It's supposed to be soothing," he explained. "It might help your session."

"Thanks," I replied, sipping the floral tea. I wasn't sure if I liked it, but I was willing to try anything to feel better.

"Annabeth," Dr. Andrews announced as she opened the door to her office. She was so regal with her tall stature and perfect posture. However, she was so warm and kind in sessions that I was able to speak freely without fear that I would disappoint her. She was an excellent therapist.

"Thanks for seeing me on such short notice," I squeaked out, setting the teacup on the table.

"I'm happy to have you. Now, have you decided if you'd like to try hypnotherapy?"

I nodded quickly. "Yes, I think it's important to give it a try."

"Very good," she said. "Let's go into this room," she said, gesturing toward a door I had never entered before. "It's better for this type of treatment."

I followed her into a room far different from her typical office. The lights were dim and soft ocean sounds played from surround sound speakers. There was just one armchair in the room, next to a blanket and pillow on the floor.

I looked to her for direction, suddenly feeling silly for requesting something out of the norm.

"Go ahead and take your shoes off," she said. "Do

whatever you need to do to make yourself completely comfortable. Then, lie down on that mat."

I slipped my flats off and placed them beside the blanket. Then, I got onto the mat, surprised by how weightless I felt on it. I didn't know what it was made out of, but I wanted one for my own home.

"Are you comfortable?" she asked.

"Very," I sighed. I wanted to drift off to sleep.

"Good. First, I want to let you know that hypnosis is not an exact science. It's somewhat controversial in our field because a lot of scientists are skeptical of its effectiveness. Now, I wouldn't normally use this kind of therapy, but you're an extreme case. Your subconscious has a way of keeping things under wraps and is very strong. Normally, I'd just allow for things to run their course with talk therapy, but as I understand, there is some urgency involved."

"Yes," I answered sleepily.

"We will try it, but do not get discouraged if you aren't able to remember anything, okay? We can always try again later."

"Okay," I repeated.

"Now, I want you to imagine that you're standing on top of a flight of stairs with ten steps. I'm going to count down, and whenever I reach the next number, I want you to imagine yourself stepping down to the next step. Do you understand?"

"Yes," I murmured.

"With each step, you are going to relax your body a little bit more. Ready?"

"Yes," I whispered, already entranced by her soothing voice and the comfortable floor.

"Ten," she counted. I closed my eyes and let my face relax. My lips parted ever so slightly.

"Nine." I consciously felt my limbs go heavy and sink further into the floor.

"Eight." I noticed my breathing had already slowed and my heart beat in a steady rhythm.

I don't remember much after that. I think my mind went into autopilot around five or six. However, I wasn't completely asleep. My ears could hear her speaking to me, but the rest of me felt like I was underwater.

"Can you hear me?" she asked.

"Yes," I replied.

"I want you to go back to your honeymoon. You've just gotten in the car with your new husband and you're on your way to your accommodations. I'd like for you to go there and just take in the sights, smells, sounds, and feelings."

While I was typically reluctant to remember those times, my inhibitions felt lower, as if I were drunk. I allowed myself to sit in the car beside Greg as he drove down the highway.

I remembered the smell of his car. He'd bought it about a month before the wedding, much to my chagrin. I thought it was too expensive of a purchase to be making so close to our wedding. But I liked it better than his old truck that hardly worked. This one hummed quietly and smelled like a new car. I sipped a soda as we cruised down the sunny highway, not a care in the world.

When we stopped to get gas, I got out of the car and stretched my legs. My feet were still sore from the previous night. I was never much of a dancer, but as the bride, it was my duty to at least stand on the dance floor. I don't think we left the reception until one in the morning.

"Want anything from the store?" I yawned, sleepy from sitting in the car for so long.

"I'd take some trail mix, if you're offering," he said with a wink.

I grinned back at him. He was truly irresistible. I watched him for a moment as he lifted the nozzle to the tank. His biceps bulged under his short sleeves. I had the urge to go up behind him and wrap my arms around his slim waist. Later. There would be time for that later.

After a little browsing, I grabbed a few snacks and paid for them, along with the tank of gas. Then, we got back in the car and continued toward our cabin. Greg blasted the radio and sang loudly. He was totally tone deaf, which made it all the more endearing.

I reached over and ran a hand through his blond hair. I felt like we hadn't been alone for months. When we were, we were always working on wedding plans. We'd try to have a date night, only to end up fretting over our choices for the wedding registry and reception dinner. He had his heart set on prime rib, while I preferred chicken. In the end, we served both.

In the days leading up to the wedding, we decided that it might be fun to spend some time apart so that we were more excited when we were finally together. I think we made it about a day before we were sick and tired of our nagging parents and needed to blow off a little steam. However, we seemed to be flanked by friends and family at all times. Finally, we were truly alone together, and it felt amazing. We had nearly a week of vacation time before we planned on moving into our new apartment together. As a wedding gift, our friends planned on moving all of our things from our respective homes into the new apartment while we were away. The deposit and the first month of rent were already paid for. We truly didn't have a single thing to worry about while we were away. I hardly knew what to do with the freedom!

"This guy had better get off my ass before I brake

test him," Greg sneered, using the tough guy persona that he'd earned in the military.

I rolled my eyes. Greg was as gentle as they came. I knew he wasn't about to do something stupid to the guy who was tailgating us.

"Yeah, and end up with damage to your brand-new car," I said dryly. "Calm down, babe. He'll pass us eventually. If I miss out on a second of our vacation because you're having a pissing match with a stranger, I'm not going to be happy."

"Yes, dear," he said sweetly as he slowed his pace to allow the car behind him to go around him. However, the car slowed down the same amount, still following much too close for comfort.

I looked back in the rearview mirror and thought it was strange that this car wouldn't pass us. There were several opportunities to, but it never did. I even turned around at one point, wondering if the driver was elderly or just really young and inexperienced. I saw the face of a large man with short hair but couldn't really make out any other features. The car was a brown sedan, though. I remembered thinking that it was a really ugly color for a car. I much preferred Greg's shiny black car.

I jolted up from the mat, my breathing fast and panicked. I looked wildly around the room, expecting to see my attacker there with me. Instead, I saw a concerned Gloria staring back at me.

"What did you experience?" she asked, keeping her voice calm and steady.

"I—I saw the car," I stammered.

"What car, Annabeth?"

"There was a car that followed Greg and me on our honeymoon. I remember it because it was so close to us. It never turned away, even when we were on the back road going into our cabin."

"And you're sure this was your attacker?" she asked.

"What did it look like?" Gloria asked, looking excited.

"It was a brown sedan. Very plain, kind of ugly," I added. "There was absolutely nothing special about it, other than the fact that it was following us too closely."

"Very good," Dr. Andrews said, looking impressed. "That's a tremendous discovery. Do you remember the driver?"

I squeezed my eyes shut, but the flashback was already gone. I shook my head warily.

"That's okay," she said. "You've already made tremendous strides."

"I know it was a man," I said, thinking hard. "I never got a good look at his face. I think he was average-sized, maybe a little bigger than average. He had short hair. I don't think there was anything about him that made him stand out—just like his car."

"So you saw a very average-looking man?" she asked. "That's helpful. That will eliminate certain suspects. That's still very good information."

I nodded. I didn't feel like I remembered much, but it was better than nothing. At least I had a car. I felt pretty confident about that.

"You're shaking," my therapist noted. "Are you feeling okay?"

"Yeah," I breathed. "Can we try this again? I feel like I'm getting really close to remembering him. I saw the day of my honeymoon so clearly. If you can help me get to the maze, I think I could find him. I want to try."

Dr. Andrews took off her glasses and cleaned the lenses on her blouse. "I don't doubt that you could regain some lost memories. However, I think it's too much for one day. Minds are extremely fragile. If I push too hard, you might break, and then it will take much longer to get to where we want to be."

"When can I see you next?" I asked.

"Let's try the day after next. I'll schedule you for a longer time slot in the morning. Until then, I want you to get lots of rest and try not to overexert yourself. Take your medication if you need it, but don't overdo it. Put yourself in whatever situation you need to feel safe."

"Thank you," I said. "I'll see you then."

I rushed back to my car after setting my appointment time with the receptionist. I didn't even double-check to make sure I was in line with the security cameras as I walked to my car. After locking the doors behind me and inserting the key into the ignition, I scrambled in my purse for my phone.

My hands were shaking so badly that it took me three tries to type out the text message to Detective Reyes. When I pushed *Send*, I breathed a sigh of relief. Finally, I was able to provide some information that could be used in the case. I had a very strong feeling that the owner of the car was directly responsible for my misery. My memory had its faults, but I saw it so clearly it was as if I was watching a film about my life.

Before I even left the parking lot, I had a message from Gabriel.

Awesome work. This helps a lot. I'll begin looking up every brown vehicle that was licensed in this county before you were held captive. I'll let you know if I find anything interesting.

My chest fluttered at this praise. Now, I just had to find a way to keep myself safe and occupied for another day and a half before I could see my therapist for another hypnosis session.

Not wanting to go home, I drove straight for the hospital to see my brother. I knew that he probably would be pretty out of it from the medications he was on, but I figured it was best if I surrounded myself with others. And, while I was mortified that my mom was asking about increased security around my brother, it might be nice to have a few extra eyes watching out for me.

CHAPTER TWENTY-ONE

I showed up to my second hypnotherapy session almost a whole hour early. The receptionist looked confused when he saw me before my appointment time, but he offered me the standard cup of tea beforehand.

"Yes, please," I said eagerly, trying to prepare myself for the session in any way that I could. I chugged it down and was given a refill a short while later. In an attempt to stay calm like Gloria suggested, I began to flip through a magazine on her coffee table. It was one of those home improvement magazines that showed the reader all of the ways their home was deficient. I read up on ways to organize the kitchen by purchasing a whole bunch of different storage containers. Then, I read that cold water is best for cleaning blood stains and that ink could be removed with hairspray. I thought this was common knowledge.

Then, I got to a page that explained how to build a brick wall for a backyard patio. I closed the page right there. I didn't need to know how easy and fun it was to stack bricks to create walls. I didn't want to imagine some guy sitting in his basement, gleefully constructing a maze to torture innocent people.

Fortunately, Dr. Andrews finished up with her patient ahead of schedule, and I was allowed to enter her meditation room early. I really enjoyed the space. It made me feel relaxed, which was no easy task. I took a deep breath, inhaling whatever fragrant essential oils she diffused into the air. The soft light and the soothing sounds made my body feel a little heavier as I took my place on the ground. By the time she entered the room to begin, I had nearly sent myself into a trance.

"How have you been feeling since our last session?" she asked.

"Anxious to get back here," I replied quickly. "I tried to obtain helpful information from my brother, but his memory hasn't been recovered."

"How is he doing?" she asked.

I bit my lip. "Not great," I admitted. "We figured he'd be ready to start his physical therapy, but he's still pretty weak and woozy. They're making sure he doesn't have an infection from his wound. I tried to talk to him yesterday, but he wasn't feeling very well."

"I'm sorry to hear that. Have you heard any updates about your case?"

I shook my head. "Not really. The detective assigned to our case has been trying to find information on every brown sedan owner in the county. I guess there are a lot more than we assumed. Besides that, there are no other leads."

"How does that make you feel?" she asked.

I thought hard to come up with an apt description of every emotion that had been running through my exhausted brain. In just a short week, I'd had my son taken from me, my brother was seriously injured, and my stalker was closer than ever before. And my mom was in therapy and partially blamed me for this mess. Things really couldn't get much worse.

I sighed. "Completely helpless."

"Your being here to work on memory recovery is a lot," she said firmly. "Don't forget about the people who are here to help you."

"Okay," I said weakly, feeling like a child.

"So, are you ready to begin? I know you had a breakthrough last time, but I feel the need to warn you that you might not get such dramatic results every time.

Like I said, this is not an exact science. I want you to open your mind up to the possibility that you can unlock the door to your subconscious, but I don't want a lack of results to throw away the key. Understand?"

"Yes, I understand," I responded, eager to get started.

"Then let's begin." She smiled warmly. "Take a moment to relax. Again, picture yourself at the top of a stairwell. Once you reach the bottom, your mind will be ready to explore everything that's been hidden away for so long. Ten."

I began to soften just as I had the last time. This time, I didn't remember hearing the number seven before I was out. However, I remained aware enough to listen to the doctor's suggestions.

"Today, I want you to place yourself inside the maze. You are simply a visitor, trying to observe whatever you're able to find. You are not in danger. No one can hurt you now. You are simply walking through, as if you are in a museum of your memory. You will see through the eyes of your past self, but you can leave whenever you want to. What do you see?"

I walked into the maze, allowing my fingers to brush against the cold brick. The awful smell returned to me, the dank, humid stink filling my nostrils.

"It's dark," I said. "It smells so bad."

"Can you describe it to me?" Dr. Andrews asked.

I inhaled a few times. "It has the mustiness of my grandma's old house. It kind of smells like dirt or dust."

"Anything else?"

I sniffed again. "Body odor. It's a man who hasn't showered or has been sweating. It's not a nice musk, either," I said, remembering how I strangely liked the scent of Greg's dirty shirts at the end of a long day.

"If you had to guess, where do you think you are? Is it a warehouse, or perhaps a cabin? Is it the main level of an old farmhouse?"

"It's underground," I said with certainty. "The ground is soft in some places. There are spiders—those small, spindly ones. I think I'm in a basement. Sometimes, I hear footsteps over my head. That's when I try to hide."

"That's good. Now, how big is the space? Walk around and try to get a sense of it."

I took a cautious step forward, my hands outstretched. I took a few steps until I hit a wall.

"I don't know," I said frantically. "I don't know how to get around."

"Place your right hand on the wall," Gloria said gently. "Walk alongside the wall."

I did as she said, making turns around the maze. I found a few familiar dead ends, then returned to what I believed was my starting point.

"I'm not great with measurements," I said.

"Compare it to something. Is it bigger or smaller than a football field?"

"Maybe a little bigger," I guessed. "But if it is, it's not by much."

"That's good. That's very good," she said, encouraging me. "Now, who do you think could build a maze like this?"

I ran my hands over the stone walls. "Someone who has a mind for design," I concluded. "He is strong enough to lift the heavy bricks and stones by himself. He likes to be alone."

"Why?" she asked.

I didn't have an immediate answer for her. I had a strong suspicion the guy was a loner freak, but I couldn't come up with the evidence to support it.

"I don't know," I said, my voice falling.

"That's fine," she said. "We can come back to it. What does his voice sound like when he talks to you?"

"It's deep and angry," I said quickly. Even my conscious self remembered that.

"What kinds of things does he say to you?"

I squeezed my eyes shut even tighter. I heard the words, but they all came through in my voice.

"He tells me that I'm pretty and that I belong to him. I ask if I can leave and he just laughs at me. He doesn't care if I cry. He thinks it's a fun game. If I don't do what he wants, he gets angry and calls me bad names. He says I'm a slut who needs to be taught a lesson."

"How does he teach you a lesson?" she asked.

My breathing became more fast and shallow. "He takes my clothes off and touches me. Sometimes, he grabs my hand and makes me touch him. His skin is always hot and sweaty. He also forces himself on me. I cry and scream because it hurts, and I can't breathe."

"You're being very brave," the therapist said. "I want you to take a step back and breathe for a moment. "You're doing a great job."

With her guidance, I was able to quiet my mind and slow my breathing down to the point where I felt like I was in a dream again.

"Annabeth, I'm going to ask you to do one more thing before we're done here," she said. "I want you to walk around until you find him."

"No," I said almost reflexively. "I can't."

"I want you to try," she persisted. "Remember, he can't hurt you. He is not allowed to touch you or talk to you. He cannot see you. He cannot harm you in any way. Find him."

"Okay," I said breathily as I continued through the maze. Suddenly, I filled with dread as the familiar scent of body odor flooded my nostrils. "He's here," I cried.

"Good work," she said. "Now, describe what he looks like to me."

I stared straight in front of me, but I couldn't see much.

"It's too dark," I whimpered.

"Turn on the light," she said simply.

Suddenly, we were standing beneath harsh fluorescent lighting. He towered over me, his heavy breathing louder than my own.

"Can you describe him?" the therapist asked.

"He's big—taller than me. He has broad shoulders and a gut," I said, my voice wavering. "Yeah, he's kind of overweight. Like the size of my brother, but fatter."

"Good. What else can you tell me about him?"

I focused hard. "He has big callused hands."

"He must work with his hands a lot."

"That's right," I said. "I hate how they scratch me when he touches me. There's dirt under his fingernails."

"What else? Look toward his face."

I looked up, but I was having a hard time distinguishing any facial features.

"His hair is messy," I concluded. "It's balding a bit in front and it's always greasy when I see him. It's the color of Gregory's hair, but kind of different. I don't know how to describe it."

"We can call it orange or red," she suggested. "Does he have facial hair?"

I didn't so much see it as I felt it across my face when he tried to kiss me. "Scratchy stubble," I answered. "It hurt."

"Now, I know that it can be hard to describe facial features, but I'll try to talk you through it. What can you tell me about his face?" Dr. Andrews asked gently.

I wasn't sure how to respond. When I looked at the figure in front of me, he was faceless. It was like pixilation censoring out something too obscene for my eyes to see.

"I can't see his face," I said, feeling exhausted. "It's just not there. He doesn't want me to see it."

"Why not?" she asked curiously.

"Because it's his biggest secret," I replied, astonished by the words that were coming out of my mouth. I felt like I was listening to another person speak about what was going on in my head. "If I saw his face, then I would know who he was. I could never love him if I knew his secret. He needs me to love him. I know that I never will."

I took a few deep breaths, but the face was still as blurry as it had always been.

"Is it getting any clearer?"

"No," I mumbled. "I can smell his breath now. It

smells like stale coffee. He used to talk so close to my face."

"Focus on the eyes. What color do you see? Does he wear glasses?"

I tried to stare him in the eyes, but the picture wasn't any clearer. "I don't think I've ever looked at his eyes. If it wasn't dark, I was looking down. I didn't want to look at him."

"That's completely understandable. Is there anything else you can tell me about him?"

I searched him over, but there was nothing left to be said that I hadn't already described. My brain felt like mush and there was nothing more I could do. I was so close to finally seeing his face, but there was something stopping me. I wanted to identify him, but I just couldn't.

"I can't do it," I whimpered, feeling broken.

"That's okay. If it's all right with you, I'm going to bring you out of it. Are you ready?"

"Yes," I cried.

"This time, you're going to go up the steps. With each step, you're going to feel more awake, more connected to the present. With each breath, congratulate yourself for working so hard and doing such a good job. When you reach the top, I want you to feel alive and refreshed."

I listened to the therapist count from one to ten, all

the while pulling myself out of the dark maze. By the time I reached the top of the imaginary stairs, my eyes were open. I sat up and looked toward the floor.

"How do you feel?" she asked.

"Like I have unfinished business," I replied, feeling confused. "Why can't I see his face?"

"It's a process," she answered. "We can keep working on it if you wish."

"I know him, though," I said. "I feel like I know him, anyway. I've spent enough time in that maze with him that I should be able to tell you much more. For some reason, I just can't do it. It's like all the answers are on the tip of my tongue, but I can't spit them out."

"Don't be hard on yourself about it," Dr. Andrews said. "You've provided me with a lot of information. If you'd like, I'd be happy to make a copy of my notes and give it to you. The police might be able to make use of it."

"Actually, that would be nice," I replied, thinking about how impressed Detective Reyes would be with me if I had a list of facts for him.

"I'll be right back," she said, rushing out of the room. I got up and slipped my shoes on as I walked around the small room. I knew that it would only be a matter of time before I could identify my stalker, but I worried that by the time my brain cooperated, it would be too late. My son didn't have a lot of time, and for all

I knew, my stalker could snatch me off the street at any point.

Dr. Andrews returned with a printed copy of her handwritten notes. As I read them over, I was surprised by what they said.

"I really said these things?" I asked.

"I wrote it down verbatim," she answered. "I know it can seem kind of foreign to you, but the subconscious memory is a strange place."

"Can I accept this as truth?" I asked, holding up the paper.

"I think so. If you're asking if it would hold up in a court of law, I'm not certain about that. But I have reason to think that what you saw is accurate. Anyway, it doesn't hurt to have the police take that into consideration."

"Can we do this again?" I asked. "I think I'm making some serious progress."

"Let's try again early next week," Gloria said, checking her schedule. "Why don't you come in first thing on Monday morning? Until then, get lots of rest and use some of the coping mechanisms we talked about in our previous sessions."

"Okay," I replied, feeling as if I had been up all night. "Thank you for your help. I'll see you Monday."

Though I left the office with documentation that I was able to conjure up a memory of my stalker, I still felt like something big was missing. It was more than just a few facial features, too. There was a big piece to the puzzle that I was blanking on. Unfortunately, I didn't know where to begin when it came to figuring it out. I was putting together a puzzle with missing pieces and no picture to go on, and time was running out.

CHAPTER TWENTY-TWO

After an attempt at a nap, I got up to find numerous missed calls from my mom. As it turned out, Tom had developed pneumonia during his hospital stay and had been sent back to the ICU. As I drove to the hospital to meet my mom, I pounded at my steering wheel with rage. If Tom died because of my stalker, I would never forgive myself. My mom would never forgive me either.

The receptionist at the front desk handed me a visitor's badge the second I came through. "Room 443," she said, clearly aware of who I was.

"Thanks," I said hurriedly as I ran up the stairs toward his room.

When I got there, my mom was standing outside

his room, looking through the window. She clutched wadded tissues in her hand as she sniffled.

"Mom?" I said cautiously, ready to hear the worst.

"I was told that he's going to be okay, but it doesn't always look that way," she cried. "It's scary to see him connected to so many tubes and wires."

"I know," I replied, feeling my stomach drop. He looked so weak and frail—nothing like the Tom I knew. "How did this happen? He looked fine yesterday."

"These things just happen," my mom sighed. "He had a knife rip through his body. It does unspeakable damage. It's not like you're neatly punching a hole though a body—it completely rips apart tissue and breaks bone. When your body is already weak, it's easy for infection to set in. Unfortunately, it can be really dangerous, especially when he already has a hole in his back."

"But he's going to recover, right?" I asked.

"That's what they tell me. There are no certainties when it comes to these matters," she said, staring into Tom's room. "I've seen it before—one day, you're getting ready to discharge someone, and the next day, they're in the morgue."

"Don't be so morbid," I scolded her. "He's an otherwise healthy guy. He'll pull through."

"I think so too," she said. "It's just never good to be in the ICU. It's never good."

"Well, can I at least go inside and talk to him?" I asked. "Maybe it'll help if he knows that we're here for him."

"We're not allowed in," she said. "His immune system is too fragile right now. They're pumping him full of antibiotics and draining the fluid from his lungs. If we were allowed in, I'd be right by his side, just like I was after you were found. Do you remember that?"

I gritted my teeth. I didn't remember.

"No, of course not," she said dismissively. "If you need to be somewhere, you can go. I'll tell him you stopped by when I'm allowed to go in."

"I don't need to be anywhere," I lied, pushing the paper from Dr. Andrews's office deeper into my pocket.

"Well, there's not much you can do here now. I just wanted you to know what was going on with Tom. I can call you if there are changes in his condition."

"Okay," I replied softly, aware that I was not wanted nor needed. "I think I'll head over to the police station and see if there are any leads. I'll be back later."

My mom didn't respond but continued to look at my brother, her hand clutched to her chest. I blew Tom a kiss and took off down the hall to escape the hospital as quickly as possible. The winding halls of the hospital often felt like the subterranean maze, though this one was too sterile.

I marched into the police station, blowing right past the guy working the front desk. They also knew who I was. I was becoming a regular in places where I didn't want to be a regular. In the past week, I had been to my therapist, the hospital, and the police station more times than I could count.

"Annabeth," Gabriel exclaimed, surprise in his voice. "I didn't know you were coming. Is something wrong?"

"No more than usual," I replied. "Can we talk?"

"Sure," he said, looking around the precinct. "Just give me a minute. I have to file a few reports and then I'll be right with you. Can I get you something to eat or drink? What do you want?"

"Oh, whatever you're having," I said, waving my hand as if to say that I didn't want him to put any effort into it.

"Okay. You can sit in here, and I'll be right back."

He ushered me into a small office, not much larger than a walk-in closet. I looked around, taking advantage of the time alone. When we spoke before, it was always in an interrogation room. I crept around the room and found framed photos on a shelf. Two of them were school photos of his young daughters. They were absolutely gorgeous and looked just like Gabriel. The next one was a family photo that made my heart sink. The family of four posed in front of massive pumpkins at a pumpkin patch. It looked like a Christmas card photo. Gabriel's wife was stunningly beautiful and had a dazzling smile. The happiness they exuded in the photo was far greater than anything I could remember. I had amazing moments with Gregory Jr., but they were always bittersweet without my late husband.

From looking at the pictures, I assumed that Gabriel was still madly in love with his deceased wife. There was no way you could stop loving a woman who looked like that. She had died in the last few years, too, so the wounds were still fresh. Someone like Gabriel could probably get any woman he wanted. He would be okay in the end.

"Hey, sorry about that," he said, poking his head into the doorway. I jumped, worried that he caught me snooping. "I'm all yours. I grabbed a few bagels and coffees from the break room. Will you have one with me?"

I sat down across from his desk and scooted my chair a little closer. I still didn't have much of an appetite, but when he put it that way, I couldn't refuse. I grabbed a plain bagel, split it in half, and smeared a thick layer of strawberry cream cheese on each face. I only took small sips of coffee in an attempt to keep my anxiety at bay. I'd have to call Dr. Andrews's office and ask the receptionist what kind of tea he made.

"So, you said that you have something to tell me,"

he said as he chewed. "Is it good news? I could use some good news."

"I could too," I replied. "I'm not sure how to classify it. I've been seeing my therapist lately, and we decided to give hypnotherapy a try. It's been scary, but I think I've regained some memories."

"Really? Is that how you remembered the brown sedan?" he asked, sitting up a little straighter. "How does it work?"

"I'm not exactly sure, but I think that she hypnotizes me and guides me through questions about my past. When I imagine certain memories, it feels like I'm actually there."

"And you're remembering things you didn't previously remember?"

"I think so," I said with less confidence than I had when I left the sessions. "I don't remember a lot about what I say or see when I'm out, but my therapist has been keeping detailed notes. I thought I'd show them to you. In the first session, I only remembered the brown car. In the second one, I tried to remember the maze and my stalker."

"Yeah, that sounds really useful," he said, taking the papers from me. He scanned them for a moment, the tip of his tongue sitting between his front teeth as he read.

"Do you know what?" he said, a smile forming on

his face. "We have a sketch artist we use with these kinds of cases. I can send him this description and see what he comes up with."

"It's not a very good description," I said sheepishly.

"It's good enough," he replied. "It's also important for the profile to know that the guy likely built the maze himself. Do you have reason to believe that this is factual?"

I shrugged. "It's all I have. I understand if you don't believe me. I know that I'm not a very credible witness."

"No, you're providing a lot of good information. I just wish we could do more."

He looked toward the desk, as if he were afraid to make eye contact with me. My stomach churned.

"What do you mean?" I asked, my voice wavering.

"I'm afraid I have some bad news for you," he sighed. He looked distraught, which only sank my hopes even lower. "It's Morrie."

"He's dead," I interjected. "He shouldn't be a problem. Besides, I'm almost a hundred percent sure he's not my stalker. That guy couldn't build a maze if he tried. And I'm fairly certain my attacker has pale skin and light hair. It's not Morrie. I get why you wanted to pin a pedophile, but I don't think he has anything to do with this."

"I'd have to agree with you there," Gabriel said.

"Unfortunately, my captain thinks there's reason to believe that he took your son. I've been close to the case for a few days now, so I think we're looking for a completely different type of person. But if you're the captain of a precinct and a known pedophile kills himself after being brought in for questioning, that raises a lot of red flags. Sometimes, when there's a lot at stake, it can be hard to see past that. When you're in charge, there's a lot of pressure to make a call. Sometimes, it might not always be correct."

"Where's the pressure coming from?" I asked frantically. "I'm the one with the missing child and a stalker after me. I'm the pressure, am I not?"

Gabriel sighed deeply and sat back in his chair. "Let's pretend for a moment that you're a month in the past. Your son is safe, and your stalker has not been in contact with you for years. For all you know, he's dead. Now, how would you feel if you saw in the news that a pedophile was suspected of kidnapping a young boy?"

"Pretty scared," I admitted, trying to follow his line of thinking.

"Exactly. A lot of people would not hesitate to demand the maximum sentence, even if this guy wasn't charged with the kidnapping. So, imagine what people would do if they found out that the pedophile was being set free."

"Outrage," I said softly.

"Precisely. Now, in our case, the creep is dead. If you're in charge of making people feel safe, you want to assure your public that the risk is gone. He could release a statement saying that the prime suspect is dead, but the child is still missing. That way, the town can organize a search party for the child and it will bring everyone together. It's a big, feel-good moment when the boy is found safe and sound."

I was having a hard time comprehending his hypothetical statements. I couldn't pretend a child was missing when my Gregory was being held by a freak.

"This isn't just some random kid we're talking about," I said, raising my voice. "This is my son. He's the only one I've got. He's the only living memory I have of my husband. If I lose him, them I might as well let the guy just take me. Nothing will matter anymore. How can you give up on this case?"

My hands started to tremble and my face felt hot. I wanted to pick up my bagel and coffee and throw them at the wall, but I remembered I was in a police station and my case was already being dumped off onto a citizen search party. I wasn't exactly a pillar in the community, either. I wasn't sure if anyone would even show.

"I'm not giving up on the case," he said, "but I don't have the support of my precinct. I've been working on it pro-bono since last night. I'm trying to give it the full attention it deserves, but I've been given more cases in the meantime," he said, slapping a stack of folders on his desk.

"How do you expect to have the time to work at night?" I asked. When I gave him a closer look, he did seem very tired. There were light purple bags underneath his dark brown eyes.

"That's the problem," he said warily. "I'm a single dad. I really hate having to hire someone to raise my girls. If I'm lucky, I'll make it home by bedtime so I can kiss them goodnight. Then, I work while they sleep. If I'm lucky, I'll get a few hours of rest before I have to get them ready for school. Sleep deprivation doesn't help detectives, either. I'm really trying my best, but I just wanted you to understand why progress might seem slow. You've brought in a lot of good information, but we don't have a bunch of people working on it now. You've got me, and whatever assistants I can rope into doing a little under the table work for me."

"That's not fair to my son," I cried.

"I know," he said gently. "I know it's not."

"Then why don't you stand up to your boss?"

He sighed. "There's one police station in town. If I get fired, I'll have to move. That means I'll have to uproot my daughters from the only home they ever knew and take them somewhere else. In the meantime,

I'll have to search for a new job so I can afford to take care of my kids."

I stared at the floor. It was over. My son would never be found unless I found him myself. Before long, I would be kidnapped, too, and there would be no one to search for me. Suddenly, I had an idea.

"Would the case be reexamined if I suddenly went missing?" I asked, rage embedded in my tone.

"Oh, come on," Gabriel said exasperatedly. "Are you saying that you'd allow yourself to become bait in order for the police to take notice?"

I didn't like seeing him angry, especially with me. "I don't know," I backpedaled. "It's just another hypothetical, you know?"

"Annabeth," he said, reaching across his desk to grab my hands. "Please don't do anything to harm yourself," he begged. "I'm serious about this. Your stalker wants to complete the set. As long as he's working on grabbing you, your son should be safe and he'll stop leaving us little hints. We need you on the outside if we want to find your son. If he has you, then we may never recover the two of you. Do you understand that?"

I nodded.

"Good," he replied sternly. "I have to go interview suspects for another case now. If you have any information, please come to me first. I'm still working on the case, even if no one around here knows that," he said softly.

I got up from my seat and stormed out of his office without saying another word. On my way out to the parking lot, I made sure to glare at every single police officer who crossed my path. A morbid thought popped into my head that I couldn't shake. I was under a lot of stress and usually wasn't so rude, but I couldn't help myself. I was fuming.

"I hope you have fun recovering my dead, violated body," I spat. "I guess I'll see you all then."

CHAPTER TWENTY-THREE

Once I had calmed down from my talk with Gabriel at the police station, I was mortified with my behavior. They had let my child and me down, but I was making myself very unlikeable. Typically, that wouldn't faze me much, but I needed a favor from them. If Gabriel was upset with me, he might not work as hard on my case, seeing as he really didn't have to work on it at all.

Sorry for the drama at the police station yesterday, I texted him. *I've been under a lot of stress, but that's still no excuse for my behavior. I'm glad you're still trying to help my son. I hope you still want to help after I was so rude to you.*

I received a message back instantly, though I

waited a few minutes to read it as I mustered up the courage.

Don't worry about it. I understand. Do you have any more leads?

I wish I did. I'm going to talk with a friend who knows some stuff about construction. Maybe he knows something that could help us.

Good luck, he responded. *Stay safe.*

My heart lurched in my chest. How was it possible that he still cared about my wellbeing after I was such a terror in his office? While I didn't understand, I was extremely grateful to have him working on my case.

Remembering what Jacob had told me earlier in the week about his new job, I decided that he might have some insight into who my stalker was. I was impressed with Gabriel's profile, but it didn't seem complete. Otherwise, it would have been fairly easy to catch the guy, right? I just had this feeling that one little puzzle piece would crack the case wide open. I only had to tip one more domino for all the others to fall into place.

I drove down the dusty road to his most recent construction site. Jacob had worked with computers for years before he discovered that he could use his software to do architectural work. When he explained it to me, I thought it was rather brilliant. It kind of seemed like he was cheating the system, but that was the way that technology sometimes worked. If he could find a cheaper and more efficient way to do things, then he might as well give it a shot.

Somehow, Jacob managed to create a database, of sorts, that stored blueprints of just about any building in the public record. Then, designing a new place was just as simple as clicking a few features and letting the computer plan the rest. He could even 3-D print building components with the software. He needed a few hired hands to piece the building together, like a Lego house, but it was simpler and cheaper than your typical construction crew. Apparently, he was making good money and didn't have to work that hard. I only wish I would have thought of the idea first.

When I pulled up to the site of the new community center, I saw a bunch of guys resting around a water cooler. Realizing I was in the presence of a lot of builders, I clutched my pepper spray in my hand, tucking it inconspicuously into my pocket.

"Do—do you know where Jacob is?" I squeaked, suddenly afraid that he wasn't at the site.

"He's in there," a burly guy said, pointing to a trailer office.

I nodded my head at the construction worker and dashed into the office.

"Annabeth!" Jacob exclaimed, his ruddy face turning a shade brighter. "What are you doing here?"

"Sorry," I said hastily. "Is this a bad time? I just wanted to talk to you about something."

"No, not at all." He grinned. "I just wasn't expecting you. Are you okay? You look rattled."

I shook my head. "Just a little jumpy these days. Ever since I realized that my stalker is probably a construction worker, I've been nervous around those types."

"Those guys out there?" he asked. "If one of them lays a finger on you, I'll kill them. You don't need to be afraid when I'm around."

"Okay," I said softly.

"Can I get you something?" he asked. "You look like you're wasting away."

"No, I'm fine," I responded.

"I'll get you coffee," he insisted, retreating to the kitchenette at the back of the trailer. I picked up the newspaper from his table and began to flip through the pages. I saw an article about Morrie and it sent fresh waves of anger through me. I couldn't help but think of all the naïve mothers out there who were so relieved to have a convicted pedophile off the streets. Only I knew that the danger was still out there.

"Here ya go," he said brightly, setting a cup in front of me.

"Aren't you having one?" I asked.

He shrugged. "Already had mine for the day. So, what's on your mind?"

I tried to think of the best way to word what I was thinking. I knew that if I gave Jacob too much information, he'd take it upon himself to solve the crime. After all, he said that he had too much free time on his hands these days. I certainly didn't want to tell him that the police had all but given up on me. He would probably go into a rage and cuss out the police officers. It might be warranted, but it wouldn't help my case.

"The police profile suggests that my stalker could be in the construction business."

"Really?" he asked, looking interested. "And you wanted to talk to someone who knows about construction?"

"Exactly," I said, relieved that Jacob understood. "The police are having a hard time nailing down a guy who has construction skills and a motive to harm people. I guess I was wondering if you knew anyone who fits the description."

"You think I know your stalker?" he asked, looking amused. "That would be insane. Do you think that he could be right under my nose this whole time? I think I'm a little more observant than that."

"I don't know," I said warily. "I'm at the end of my rope here. I'm just trying to gather as much information as I can. Do you know anything that can help me?"

He frowned. "You poor thing. You look so tired. Really, I think that coffee will help you. If you want, you can chug it down and take a short nap on my couch. I do it all the time. You'll feel so much better and your mind will work more efficiently."

"No, that's okay," I replied. "I just came here to talk. So, do you know any workers with a dodgy past? We're not necessarily looking for someone with a felony conviction, just an anger problem or something of that nature."

He thought for a minute, scratching his head. "Not really. A lot of these guys have records, but they do good work for little money, so I have no problem with them. Do you want me to start interrogating them?"

"No," I replied quickly. The last thing I wanted was for Jacob to tip off a potential suspect. "I don't need you to do anything. I just wanted to see if you had any leads. If I showed you a picture of some construction, do you think it could help you remember a particular builder?"

"Pictures?" he asked, raising his eyebrows.

I dug in my purse for the copies of the Polaroids that Detective Reyes made for me. I hadn't looked at the photos since they arrived at my house.

"The sick son of a bitch sent me pictures of his handiwork," I replied. I found the sheet that only contained the maze and passed it to him. I deliberately left out the photos of my son and me.

"Wow," he said.

"I know," I replied. "It's awful."

"It's impressive," he said. "Hold on, I want to get my reading glasses. My eyes aren't what they used to be."

He walked away from the table and began rummaging through drawers in the back of the trailer. I took the opportunity to dump half of my coffee into the potted plant by my side. It was an old trick I had learned in my youth. I couldn't stomach the stuff at the moment, though I knew that it would be rude to keep refusing his offerings. If I had more than a few sips, my stomach would surely reject it.

He came back with large glasses on. He looked awful in them, but I wasn't going to tell him that. He was a sensitive guy, always had been.

"Let's get a closer look at this, shall we?" he said with a hint of a smile on his face. I hadn't even gotten the chance to explain what I knew about it. He was too busy mumbling to himself about the construction.

"Well, what do you think?" I asked nervously.

"It's brilliant. I mean, it's really good planning and craftsmanship. It takes a certain genius to make a maze. Was it hard to get through?"

I nodded, feeling weird about our conversation. "Yeah, I guess so."

"I bet it was terrifying. Did you feel like you were going to be trapped in there forever? Did it make you lose hope of ever seeing the outside world again?"

I frowned. "Yeah, it was the worst time of my life," I said. "I really don't like your interest in this. I think I'm going to go."

"No, no," he said hastily. "I'm sorry. I'm trying to think of contacts for you right now. I've got to know someone who is capable of something like this. Finish your coffee and I'll come up with some names for you."

I sat back in my chair and took his suggestion. I raised the cup to my lips, but I noticed something white floating around in the black coffee. I figured the cup was dirty, so I pretended to take a little sip when I noticed that Jacob was staring straight at me with a smile on his face.

"What?" I asked, feeling my phone buzz in my purse.

"Nothing," he said casually. "Who's that?"

I looked at the message. Gabriel was asking something about the brown van.

"It's my mom," I lied. I scanned the text message, unsure as to why he'd ask about the location of Jacob's parents. I typed back, telling him that they had a home in Florida.

"What does she want?" he asked. "Did you tell her that you were coming over here?" I could see him trying to peer over the top of my phone, so I discreetly tilted it toward me. I didn't want him to think that I had anything to hide, but I certainly didn't want him to catch me talking to Gabriel. Not only was he a police officer, but Jacob seemed to think that I was into him.

"No," I replied, distracted by my conversation with Gabriel. "She's updating me on my brother's condition."

We found a brown van in a shop outside of town. The mechanic said that there were bullet holes in the door and the wheel wells were bent from driving over something, like a median. It's registered to David and Cynthia Morse, but the owner is located in Florida. I believe these are your friend's parents. If so, he needs to be brought in for questioning immediately. Do you know where we can find him?

My stomach dropped. I looked up at Jacob to find him staring at me again. I couldn't let on that he was a suspect in my case or he would panic and do something drastic. I had to keep calm and continue having a casual conversation with the man who had caused a lifetime of misery for my family and me.

CHAPTER TWENTY-FOUR

My mind immediately sifted through all of his odd behavior throughout the week. He'd reappeared into my life after the kidnapping like a white knight coming to save me. When I needed support and reassurance, he'd asked me intrusive and inappropriate questions. When I asked him for expertise and showed him deeply troubling photographs, he smiled and praised the creator. He pushed food and drinks onto me, drinks with white residue floating around in the cups. Repeatedly, he asked me on dates while I was dealing with a personal crisis and got agitated when I refused him. He wanted to keep tabs on me, but not because he wanted me safe. He just wanted me alone.

I was absolutely petrified, but I couldn't let Jacob

know it. I just needed to find a way to get out of his trailer and back to the police station, anywhere to be away from him.

"How's he doing?" Jacob asked.

"Pneumonia," I replied, trying to text Gabriel back without Jacob catching on. "He's in bad shape."

"That's too bad," Jacob said. "It's a shame he had to get caught up in all of this. I don't think Tom really ever liked me. I never understood why."

"That's not true," I said, crinkling my brow. "Tom's a really nice guy. He's not the type to dislike people for no reason." I was suddenly feeling very defensive about my brother. If Tom didn't like Jacob, it was because he was being a cautious older brother. I finally understood why my mom didn't want me around Jacob as a child. He was grooming me to one day be his.

In one of my anxious, sleepless nights as a young mother, I'd made the mistake of researching child sex trafficking. Even though my son was always under the close supervision of a trusted adult, the fear of his being taken for someone else's use crept into my head. I read articles about children being trained by older adults to comply with their wishes. I was stunned by how easily children could be tricked into thinking that deviant behavior was perfectly normal and safe. Now, I realized that I was one of them. He'd made me think that I had a cool, mature friend. All the while, I was dealing with a monster who wanted me all to himself.

I felt incredibly stupid for overlooking the most obvious suspect this whole time. While I was stressing, trying to remember someone I didn't even know, the guy who had been there the entire time was being so blatant with his involvement. I was going to be kidnapped again and it was all my fault.

In my defense, I had been concussed on numerous occasions and had stress-related amnesia. My memories were as spotty and unreliable as they came. Add the amount of stress I was dealing with from having my son abducted from right in front of me and my brother in the ICU, and it was a wonder that I was even functional at all. Still, I should have seen it coming, but I didn't. I was the only one to blame. Well, besides my stalker.

Even with all the evidence stacking up against Jacob, I searched my mind for any reason why it couldn't be him. I so badly wanted it to be a horrible stranger who'd caught a glimpse of me walking down the street one day and decided to take me to act out his perverse fantasies. I wanted it to be someone who had committed other crimes and hurt other people, so when he was locked up, the world would be a safer place. Instead, it was my friend—someone I thought was looking out for my best interests. In the end, he couldn't even recognize my best interests if he tried. He could only see his.

Looking back, I knew he'd hated Greg. Greg was everything Jacob wasn't. Greg was handsome, athletic, and social. He was a brave military man who had strong morals and virtues. He was popular in his social circles and my parents loved him. Most importantly, I loved him. He meant the world to me, and I wanted to spend the rest of my life with him. I could see why Jacob wanted him out of the picture.

Even still, I couldn't understand how the man who had been so kind to me could abuse me so horribly, kill my husband, and abduct my intellectually disabled son. It was beyond evil.

The more I thought about it, the more I wanted to rip his throat out right then and there. Even if I forgot about all the harm he'd caused my loved ones, it would be justifiable to slaughter him in his work trailer. I felt memories drift into my head like the wind outside the office. I remembered the fear I felt when I woke up in a dark maze, my husband gone. I remembered his hot, foul breath in my face as he forced himself inside me. I cried in pain, having only experienced that action once in my life by a man I feared to be dead. He wasn't loving or gentle in the least. He was rough and aggressive, and it only got worse the more I resisted him. He laughed as he took my innocence and purposefully made it unbearable, though afterward, he tried to convince me that I loved every moment of it.

In the years past, he had ruined me for all other men. I couldn't go on a date without fearing that my rapist was the kind man on the other side of the dinner table. I certainly couldn't sleep with anyone, assuming that sex was directly linked to pain. I sabotaged many promising relationships because I was terrified of my life crashing down on me again. Besides, I had my son, and he was enough of a handful for me.

"Do you think he'll get better?" Jacob asked. "Does he remember anything yet?"

"Huh?" I asked, feeling dazed. Then I remembered what we were talking about. "Oh, no, he doesn't remember anything. I doubt he will. I'm just hoping he gets moved from the ICU soon so he can go home. Do you want to go see him later?" I asked, trying to convince him of anything that would keep me out of his clutches for just a while longer. "It would mean a lot to me if you did," I said flirtatiously. "We could go right now."

"Maybe later," he said cryptically, unconvinced by my doe eyes. "I have to stick around the site for just a little while longer."

He looked at me with my phone in my hands and squinted his eyes a little. "Who are you talking to now?"

"Still my mom," I lied. I texted Gabriel to tell him that I was with Jacob and asked if I should be concerned. I already knew the answer to that question.

Where are you?! Get out of there as soon as possible. Let me know where you end up. If you can, come to the police station.

I texted him the approximate location of the construction site. Because it was a new build, there weren't any city streets that led up to the place. It was also on the complete other side of town from the police station. I hoped he could find it quickly.

"What does she want?" Jacob asked, a little hostility in his voice. He knew that something wasn't right.

"She just wants to make sure I'm updated on his condition," I said, feeling more anxious by the minute. "I'm really worried about him, you know?"

"Give me the phone," he said. "You don't need to be bothered at a time like this. All she does is stress you out."

"I'm fine," I said, dropping my phone into my purse. I told Gabriel everything he needed to know to find me. All I had to do now was sit and wait.

"No, it's not fine," he said angrily, wrenching my purse away from me. He flung it toward the back of the trailer. My phone, my pepper spray, and my car keys were in there. Without them, I was completely defenseless.

"I need to go to the hospital," I said. "I told my mom that I would be there soon," I lied. "If I'm not there soon, she'll start to worry."

"Where does she think you are?" he asked quizzically.

"I told her I was coming here to talk to you," I said, wide-eyed and innocent. "She told me to have fun and that she'd keep in touch if she found out more about my brother."

"I thought you said no one knew you were here?" he asked. I didn't remember saying that in those words.

"Did I?" I giggled nervously. "I don't know what I said. My head's been all over the place. Nope, I told my mom before I got here that I was headed to talk to you about the maze. Why do you ask?"

"Nothing," he grumbled.

I looked around the trailer. Not too far from his chair sat a large kitchen knife. If I made a run for the door, he'd get to me first. If I tried to grab the knife, he'd snag it first. I heard machinery in the distance. It was loud—so loud that I doubted anyone would hear my screams. From what I could tell, the trailer sat about a quarter-mile away from the construction site. The workers wouldn't be any help to me.

I was trapped, so I needed to be smart about getting

out alive. Jacob liked games, so if I played along, hopefully, he wouldn't become too agitated. If his temper came out, I would be dead. If I played into his hands, he would at least be pleased enough to keep me intact. As much as I wanted to kick him in the crotch and spit in his face, it would not be wise. I had to give him exactly what he wanted in order to survive.

He sighed and looked at me. "I just want you to be happy, Annabeth. Nobody sees that. Your mother doesn't like me, your dead husband didn't like me, your brother doesn't like me, and I don't even think you like me."

"Of course, I do," I said, nearly crying. "Why would you ever think that? You're one of my dearest friends."

"Friends," he spat, as though it was a dirty word. "Anyone can be a friend. I waited around for you for so long, Annabeth. I've been waiting for you since the day we met."

"I was a child," I said, my voice shaking. "What could you possibly want with a child?"

"You've never wanted me, but I've always been there for you. I helped you relearn computer functions after you forgot them all. Without me, you'd be nowhere. All I wanted was to go on a date, and you couldn't even give me the courtesy of going to dinner with me."

My mouth gaped open. "Jacob, my son is missing! How am I supposed to even think about romance when I'm terrified that he's hurt? I need my son more than anything. I can't possibly exist without him."

"And I needed you," he argued. "Why can't I have what I want?"

My heart was pounding so hard I could see it pulse through my shirt. I needed to get out of the trailer. Jacob was becoming seriously agitated and I didn't want to be there when he exploded.

"I really need to go to the hospital," I said. "My mom is waiting on me. Can I get my purse back?"

He thought for a moment. I flinched as he stood up from the table. "I'll take you."

"What?"

"I'll take you to the hospital," he said, his voice uncharacteristically soft. "I should see your brother. You're right—it would mean a lot to your family if I was there."

"Really?" I asked, floored by his change of thought. If Gabriel was right about his being a psychopath, maybe that meant that he was a little narcissistic as well. Perhaps he really believed that his presence would make things better for everyone. I ran with the idea.

"Sure. I'll drive," he said, sounding dejected.

"We can both drive," I offered eagerly.

"Just let me do something nice for you, damn it!" he growled.

I backpedaled. "Okay, that would be nice. Thank you. It really means a lot to me."

I followed him out to his car, my instinct telling me to bolt. But unless the cops could arrive any sooner, it would be too easy for him to run me over in the car. Once we got to the hospital, I could get to a phone and call the police. With so many people around, he wouldn't dare try to harm anyone. I just had to keep him happy until then.

I breathed a sigh of relief when we got onto the main road. He hummed along to the music on the radio, suddenly in better spirits. I tried to play the damsel in distress all the way to the hospital, just to seal the deal.

"Maybe we could try to date when this nightmare is over," I lied, batting my eyelashes at him. "It's just been so stressful with Greg missing. If I had my baby back in my arms, I'd be so happy, I think I'd do just about anything. I'd be more open to the idea of dating then. I just wish we could find him."

"Yeah?" Jacob said, a small smile forming on his lips. He couldn't help himself. He was obsessed with me and ate up every sickly-sweet lie I had to offer. And to think, I was terrified that he wouldn't let me go. Now, he was driving me to the hospital where security guards stood at the door, just because I batted my eyelashes at him and asked nicely. If I had known that it was so easy to get what I want with him, just by flirting, I would have tried it a long time ago. I figured I could get Greg back if I played my cards right, but I could also just call the police and have them deal with it. I couldn't wait to see Jacob's dumb face from the back of a police car.

My muscles started to relax as we came within a few blocks of the hospital. I was so close to being free. Once there, I would excuse myself to go to the bathroom, then find the closest phone and call 911. Then, I would alert security to my situation. Greg would be found by the end of the day. I fidgeted with the seatbelt, eager to get there.

A police siren went off in the distance. Jacob sat up a little straighter and stared at me.

"You told your precious police officer that I was with you, didn't you? What else did you tell him?"

"What are you talking about?" I cried. I was beginning to sweat. "I haven't talked to him."

"I can go back and check your phone right now," he said, stopping at an intersection. The seatbelt pressed hard against my chest.

"We're almost at the hospital," I pleaded.

"You're playing me," he said. "I don't like that."

He spun his car around and started speeding off in

the opposite direction. I unbuckled my seatbelt and reached for the handle. But, by this time, he was speeding so fast that I was sure I wouldn't survive if I jumped.

"Where are we going?" I asked frantically.

"Home," he said firmly. "Now shut up, if you know what's good for you."

I gritted my teeth, trying hard not to cry. I knew that he was taking me to the maze—he didn't even have to say so.

I had a brief moment of hope in the terror I felt. I may be on my way to an underground maze I'd never escape, but at least I would see my son. Now, I just needed a way to make sure we both stayed alive.

I realized we were going to his house and needed to come up with a new plan. If I ran for it when we got to the driveway, he would take his anger out on Gregory. He didn't deserve that. I needed to be brave for my son.

"I don't feel good," I said.

"You're fine," he growled.

"I'm feeling really drowsy," I whined. "I really don't feel right. Did you put something in my drink?"

He raised his eyebrows, surprised that his plan was working out. "Just close your eyes and rest," he said.

"I'm scared," I cried.

"Just sleep," he said. "Everything will be okay."

I closed my eyes and slumped down in my seat,

trying to convincingly fake sleep. It must have worked, because he started humming along to the radio again. I kept my eyes shut tight, even when I felt the car lurch upward toward the garage. Finally, he stopped the car and closed his garage door behind him.

I slowed down my breathing as much as I could, practicing coping techniques that Dr. Andrews taught me. When he picked me up from the passenger's seat, I went completely limp in his arms. I kept my eyes closed and focused on his steps so I would know exactly where he was going. If he believed that I was truly unconscious, he wouldn't need to be as cautious in his attempt to cover his tracks.

Jacob carried me about ten steps into the garage before I heard him open a hatch with one hand. Then, we descended into the ground via a long staircase of wooden steps, each one squeaking underneath our weight. My brain was flooded with fear as the familiar musty scent returned to me. I fought my body to stay still when I really wanted to fight. We must have traveled two stories below the ground before he dumped me onto the cold, hard floor.

"Home, sweet home," he muttered under his breath as he rummaged through his key ring. I heard the click of the lock and something inside me told me it was time to fight for my life.

CHAPTER TWENTY-FIVE

From what I remembered of my childhood with Jacob, I knew that he liked weapons. For someone who wasn't particularly active or outdoorsy, I found this quirk quite peculiar. On his fifteenth birthday, his father had given him a fancy pocketknife that once belonged to his grandfather. He liked it so much that he was given a hunting knife the next year, in hopes that he would take to hunting like his father. However, the interest wasn't quite there. He liked to wear it on his hip but didn't care for sitting out in the cold all day, waiting for an animal to be shot down. Then, he despised how the animal smelled after being gutted and cleaned.

It wasn't that he was turned off by the killing or violence of it all. He was rather indifferent to that. He even liked the thick, juicy sausages his mom cooked up once the animal came back from being processed. However, Jacob hated spending time with the good ol' boys his father hunted with. They always ribbed on him for not having a girlfriend and teased him when he did something that was not deemed masculine.

So, after a few of these trips, Jacob quit hunting and continued to wear the knife on his person whenever he could get away with it. This was a habit that he apparently carried into his adult years, as evidenced by the top of the knife handle that dug into the side of my temple as he carried me down the stairs.

Once the lock was open, I knew that I was finally in a good position to fight. My son was on one side of me, and freedom was on the other. I just needed to remove the monster beside me.

When he wasn't paying attention to me, I jumped up and pulled the knife from the holster and stabbed it deep into his fleshy thigh. He howled in pain, shocked that I was able to harm him.

For a moment, I wish I would have aimed straight for the heart or neck, but this was a good start. From what I remember about the anatomy of the leg, there were lots of blood vessels that could cause a person to bleed out if severed. I didn't know if I hit one of them, but he seemed to be seriously disarmed for the time being. And if he wanted to stab me with that weapon, he'd have to yank it out of his own leg. If he knew anything about basic first aid, he'd realize that it could be a fatal mistake.

I made a run for it. Screaming my son's name, I went into the maze to search for him. It didn't take more than a few steps for my PTSD to kick in, rendering me a blubbering mess.

I knew that the memories of the place would mess with my head, but nothing could have prepared me for this. I needed my therapist by my side, telling me that no one could hurt me. I tried to tell myself that, but I couldn't be convinced.

The light from the top of the stairs was enough to provide me with a little insight as to where I was headed. At the very least, I could see my hand in front of my face.

"Gregory?" I called. "It's Mom. Where are you?"

I listened intently but heard nothing but Jacob's moans of pain. I kept running, hoping I would eventually run into my son. But the further I got into the maze, the harder I was hit with painful flashbacks.

As my shoulder grazed a wall, I remembered Jacob making fun of me for being so scared. He'd taunted me about my husband, saying that he wasn't so big and strong with a bullet in the back of his head. He'd imitated the sounds that Greg made as he died, mixed with his imitation of a pig squealing. I screamed and sobbed, begging him to stop, but he wouldn't. Jacob had a terrifying temper that flared up at random.

I remember crouching down beside a corner as I heard his footsteps approaching me. I wondered if it would be a good day or a bad day. On the good days, Jacob was calm and gentle and would feed me warm soup and bread. On the bad days, he was unspeakably nasty, torturing me both physically and mentally.

Of course, these moods could switch in a second. One day, he was delivering me a bowl of hot chicken broth and I'd tried to take the bowl from his hands without asking nicely. I was starving because I hadn't been fed in over a day and was on the verge of fainting. He wrenched the hot bowl from my hands and dumped the scalding liquid onto my body. From then on, I groveled at his feet whenever he was feeling benevolent.

When I reached a point in the wall that had several hooks reflecting soft light, I nearly fell to my knees. I had completely forgotten about them until then. Because I was so uncooperative whenever he was trying to sexually assault me, Jacob decided it was a good idea to string me up and tie me to the wall so it was harder to fight. He only did that once, as my ear-shattering screams were too distracting, even for him.

My hands dropped to my knees and I forced air

into my lungs so I could keep going. My head was spinning so badly that I thought I was going to pass out.

"Gregory!" I whimpered. I shouted my son's name a few more times. Finally, I heard a soft voice within the maze.

"Mom?"

Tears flooded my eyes. My baby was with me and he was alive. Suddenly, a tiny morsel of strength entered my body, just enough to keep moving. I continued through the maze, expertly navigating each turn. I was surprised that I knew where I was going. My feet guided me around the walls, completely independent of my brain.

"Mom, is that you?" a sleepy voice asked, somewhere within reach. It was the sweetest sound I had ever heard. My heart hadn't felt such joy from a sound since the day I'd heard his first cry. Though I didn't have a clue what I was doing the second he came into this world, I was overjoyed to have him. I vowed to love and protect him no matter what.

"It's me," I cried. "I'm coming for you. Keep talking, Gregory. I'm on my way."

"I'm scared," he said.

"It's going to be okay," I said, though I didn't necessarily believe it to be true. I wanted to tell him that I was scared too, but I needed him to keep calm. I had dealt with enough meltdowns in his life, and this was the last place one needed to happen.

I turned around the next corner and nearly screamed when my foot came into contact with something. I fell to my knees and wrapped my arms around my young son.

"I'm here," I repeated into his ear. "We're going to be okay."

I examined Gregory the best I could in the low light. He wasn't his usual lively self, not by any means. He was curled up in a ball on the ground, his back nestled into a corner. It was painfully familiar. He had learned how to keep himself from being startled when Jacob came through. It made my heart hurt.

He looked just like he did in the picture, but perhaps a bit thinner. His eyes were sunken and had purple circles surrounding them. I noticed that his bottom lip was split and there was some dried blood under one nostril. I wondered if Jacob deliberately took the pictures before beating him. Either way, I went into momma bear mode and was ready to rip that freak into shreds if he tried to lay a hand on my son again.

I picked him up and pulled him close to me. His skin felt so cold against mine. I rubbed his freezing arms, trying to warm him up. He flinched when I touched him.

"Are you hurt?" I asked.

"I don't know," he responded, his affect flat and emotionless.

"Are you hungry?"

"I don't know," he responded, his tone the same.

I sighed. I didn't know how to get a response out of this kid. He had been mistreated for almost a week now. Even an hour in the maze would be enough to completely shut him down. Gregory was so emotionally sensitive and hard to talk to at times. For all I knew, he had broken bones that he wasn't telling me about.

"Look," I said, feeling desperate, "I'm going to get us out of here. I need you to listen to me and do whatever I say, okay? Do you know how we used to play Simon Says when you were little? Well, I'm Simon and you're going to follow my lead, okay? It'll be like a game of hide and seek."

"We can't move," he said. "If I move, he will hurt me. If I say things that he doesn't like, he will hurt me."

"What kinds of things?" I asked, a knot in my stomach.

He shrugged. "Lots of stuff. Like, I can't ask to go to the bathroom anymore. I can't ask for food. I can't ask for my mom."

I held my son a little tighter. I could feel his slender body shivering against mine.

"Do you know how to get around the maze?" I asked.

"Yes," he said, perking up a little. "It is a very complex system, but I figured it out on the first day."

"The first day?" I asked, a small smile forming on my lips. I was so proud of my little genius. I had spent a lot of time in the maze and I didn't even know the full layout.

"I can see it in my head. We are in the top-left quadrant. The door is in the bottom-left quadrant, but it is always locked."

"Not anymore," I whispered. "The man is hurt right now. Soon, he will be too tired to even move. We are going to hide from him until he is too tired to hurt us. Then, the good guys will come and take us home. I need you to hold my hand and hide with me until that happens. Do you understand?"

"Yes, I understand," he said.

I held his hand and gave it a little squeeze. There were times when I thought I would never see him again. The police say that the first twenty-four hours are the most important when it comes to finding a missing person. Their chances of survival diminish rapidly after that first day. Even though everyone around me said that we'd find them, that statistic crossed my mind on more than one occasion.

And even though I was going to fight like hell to get

out, for a brief moment, I was just glad to be reunited with my son. There were times, especially in the early years, where I felt like I couldn't be a parent, but now I realized how primal it felt to have my child in my arms. I was meant to have him, no matter how tragic the circumstances were.

"You little bitch!" I heard Jacob scream from the door. "I'm going to kill you!"

I heard the blade of his knife scrape against the wall. The idiot had pulled it out himself. Part of me was thankful that he had—it would only make him lose blood faster. The other part was horrified that the knife would find my son or me before he took his last breath. And there was the real possibility that I had missed all vital blood vessels and had hit nothing but fat and muscle.

"You can't run from me," Jacob roared. "You're going to stay here forever, so you'd better get used to it. Don't make this harder on me. It's only going to make things harder on you and your boy—*our* boy."

I clenched my teeth. Of course he would try to tell me that my son was his progeny. Gregory was my husband's boy through and through.

I heard Jacob's pounding footsteps echoing in the maze. He was coming our way.

"Let's go," I whispered into my son's ear. "It's time to play hide and seek."

CHAPTER TWENTY-SIX

Jacob limped toward us with much more speed than I could have expected from him with an injured leg. I held my breath and looked around. He knew the maze much better than I did. Judging by the delight on his face when I showed him the pictures, he revered this place as a sanctuary. It was his greatest creation and he knew it well.

I figured there was a pretty good chance we could outrun him, but Gregory was in a weakened state. I tried to lift him up, but he was too heavy for me to carry and move quickly throughout the maze. My greatest fear was that Jacob would catch onto our movements and be able to cut us off. I would need my son's help.

"Do you hear where he is?" I whispered into Gregory's ear.

"Yes," he whispered back.

"Do you know the most logical place to go to be as far away from him as possible? Can you see our locations in your head?"

"I think so."

"Lead the way."

I know it must have seemed like poor judgment at the time, having my nine-year-old son take control of the situation. After all, I was the one who was supposed to take care of him and make sure he got out of the maze alive. Yet, I was giving him free rein to take us wherever he thought was best. Perhaps it would have been a crazy move if I had an average child with me, but Gregory was special.

At the age of three, he came home from preschool with coloring worksheets clutched in his hand. I always stuck them on the refrigerator, even though he had no interest in coloring and tended to scribble on top of the picture, just to fulfill basic requirements while still technically following directions. But on the back of this particular worksheet, Gregory had drawn an intricate maze—well, intricate for a three-year-old.

At first, the familiar nausea came forward at the sight of a maze. I wondered if he had experienced what I had endured in utero, like his brain had taken in information through mine. I knew that it was a strange thought to have, but what little kid knows how to draw a maze without being taught?

The teacher must have thought I was insane when I brought the worksheet back the next day. She had greater concerns when it came to my son, like his poor verbal skills or his ability to share with others. I could tell that she was exhausted and thought that an hour of coloring would buy her some peace and quiet, not complaints from a mom.

After some discussion, we figured out that there was a wooden maze game in the preschool. It was one of those small boards that had a wooden peg inserted along a groove, allowing a child to slide it around. It was fairly basic, something the average kid could figure out in a few minutes. The teacher said she saw Gregory using it during play time a few days prior. She concluded that he must have learned about mazes then and decided to draw one of his own. She was impressed that he had shown any creativity but was less amused by his product. To her, it looked like scribbles on a page, a creative rendering of a physical toy in the room.

But I knew that it was much more sophisticated than that. I sat down at the kitchen table with the maze and worked through it. I was a young adult, and I managed to get caught up in a few dead ends along the way. It was one of the first moments in my child's life that I knew that his gifts could get him far in life.

And at the same time, I worried that his abnormalities would work against him. Late at night, I wondered if my son was not my Greg's, but someone else's. I feared that his interest in the complicated and struggles with anything social would cause him to turn out as anything other than the polite man I was trying to raise. When we had talked about a future family, Greg really wanted a son to play sports with and to one day enlist in the military if he so desired. I just wanted a happy child.

With my hand inside Gregory's small hand, I followed him through the maze, walking as quietly as possible. Jacob was thundering behind us, screaming all sorts of profanities.

"You bitch!" Jacob roared again. "How could you do this to me? I've always been so good to you. You're nothing but a little whore. You only care about yourself."

I gritted my teeth and kept walking. I hoped my son was tuning out all the shouting. As far as I knew, he had never heard language like that before in his life.

Suddenly, Gregory changed direction, pulling me toward the left. Until that point, we had been moving in a clockwise direction. Now, we were going through a portion that I didn't remember. When I was trapped in the maze, I tried to stick to paths I knew. For a moment, I thought about taking control and returning to the path, but I had to trust my son. He was far more intuitive with these things than I was. And I had my fear tainting my decisions. He understood the social implications far less than I did. In his mind, he was working on a puzzle. Nothing else really mattered. He knew there was some danger involved, but he had no idea how bad it could be.

Jacob was near, but his footsteps slowed as he searched his creation for us.

"I'm sorry, Annabeth," he said, his voice suddenly calm and gentle. "I don't mean to frighten you. You just get me so worked up sometimes. It's only because I love you and I want us to be a happy family again. The three of us haven't been together since you were last with me. I want to prove to you that I can be a good husband and father. You mean the world to me and I'm going to make it up to you. Come out, and I'll treat you like a queen. Please, Annabeth, I mean it."

I shook my head at Gregory, trying to silently indicate that Jacob was not telling the truth. My son didn't always understand things like lies and sarcasm. He took a lot of language at face value. It made it harder for him to understand Jacob because he couldn't look at his face and see the rage.

"Don't listen to what he says," I breathed into his

ear. "He is saying bad things. You just do your maze, okay?"

He nodded and continued on through the passage, carefully stepping over bumps in the floor. He really had a good understanding of where everything was.

I tried to make some sense of how long we had been in the maze. I had hoped that Jacob would have bled out by now, but he still seemed strong enough to put up a good fight. I also knew that there was a good chance Jacob had prepared for us to fight back and knew how to trap us.

I heard what sounded like the slam of a door and nearly jumped out of my skin. Gregory didn't seem to be too perturbed and kept walking with absolute concentration. I tried to control my fast breathing and shaking limbs so I wouldn't freak him out.

"Annabeth?" I heard Jacob say, his voice so much closer than it had been before. He was gaining on us. We walked a little faster until we hit a wall.

"This wasn't here before," Gregory said frantically. I couldn't tell if he was more upset by the fact that Jacob was gaining on us or because he made a mistake. "I know this wasn't here before."

I felt the wall in front of us. It was made of wood, not stone. Jacob must have added doors to throw us off and make us easier to catch.

"Keep going," I urged my son, bile rising into my

throat. We were running out of time. I didn't know how many walls Jacob had built, but it concerned me that my son might not be able to outsmart him. He had gone from having no power over me to nothing but power over me, and it was making him crazy.

I heard another loud noise, like pounding on wood, and it made my heart leap out of my chest. It had to be another door. I just couldn't tell where it was located. It sounded like it was close to where we started, but I was becoming so turned around in the maze that I really wasn't sure which way was up.

"What the—" Jacob shouted, his voice trailing off. I paused for a moment, listening intently. Jacob sounded agitated and confused. Something wasn't going right for him. He must have made a mistake somewhere along the path. We needed to take advantage of it. But I didn't know how to explain something so intricate to my son, who continued to pull me through the maze.

"Mom, what are you doing?" he asked as I looked around. I heard the pounding sound again, followed by Jacob's voice. He sounded scared, but I had no idea what he was afraid of. I had a thought, but I couldn't pinpoint whether it was instinct or just wishful thinking.

"Can you take us back to the beginning without running into Jacob?" I asked. "We need to get to the door, but he can't get us first."

Without another word, we began walking at a brisk pace toward the start of the maze. The pounding grew louder. My stomach churned until Jacob said something that confirmed my suspicion.

"Who did you call?" Jacob whined. "Did you call the cops on me? How are we supposed to live a peaceful life if you're trying to get me in trouble?"

I gave my son's hand a squeeze. Someone was here with us. We just needed to get to the door before Jacob did. The pounding on the locked door grew louder and louder. We were going to be okay.

"Go away," Jacob roared. "If you come through that door, I will kill them both. I have a gun and I'm not afraid to fire. If I can't have them, then nobody can. We'll be together in death if that's what it takes."

I gasped. I feared that this would be a possibility, but I never thought that Jacob would be capable of killing me. I truly believed that if he looked at my face and I begged hard enough, he wouldn't be able to pull the trigger. However, I also didn't think he was capable of killing my husband, raping me, and abducting my son. There was no telling what he could do if pushed far enough.

"You don't want to do this," Gabriel's voice boomed through the wall. A small squeal came from my throat. He was here to save us. It wasn't a figment of my imagination.

"You don't know what I want," Jacob snarled, not loud enough for Gabriel to hear. He was close, clearly understanding that we were trying to get to Gabriel first.

"How close are we to the door?" I asked softly.

"Almost there," Gregory replied.

Suddenly, I felt a hand grasp my hair, tugging me so hard that my neck bent backward. I screamed as loud as I could, but a second hand hit me hard against the face. I fell to the ground with a horrible pain in my cheek. My hand went to my face and I instantly felt blood drip onto my palm.

"Shut up if you want to live," Jacob growled. The lights flashed on, and suddenly, I could see Jacob's sweaty face hovering above mine. He gnashed his teeth as he stared down at me. His entire pant leg was dark red with a rag tied tightly around the spot where I'd stabbed him. A black handgun was clenched tightly in his hand, ready to fire at a moment's notice.

"Please don't hurt us," I whimpered, thinking of my son who was standing by my side. "I'm sorry."

"I don't think that's enough," Jacob said sternly. "You deliberately disobeyed me. Now, that police officer is here and he's going to separate us. I can't have that. You know I can't have that."

I pressed a hand to the cut on my face to stem the

flow of blood while I tried to think of another plan. We were in serious trouble.

Meanwhile, the pounding on the door only got louder. It sounded like Gabriel was close to blasting the door off the hinges. I almost wanted him to stop. His presence would only aggravate Jacob even further.

But, there was nothing I could do to prevent Gabriel from doing his job. With a loud boom, the door fell flat on the floor, revealing an exhausted but satisfied Gabriel.

Jacob wasted no time in shooting him. He fired two shots squarely at Gabriel's chest, sending him to the ground. I screamed in horror, but there was nothing for me to do. Gabriel was down.

Backup would arrive eventually, but there was no telling what Jacob could do between now and then. He grabbed me by the hair again and yanked me to my feet. He had an awful grin on his face.

"Disobey me again, and your son is next. You got that?"

"Yes," I cried.

"Good. Now, take your son and get to the door. We're leaving before any more pigs can try to tear us apart. You love me, Annabeth. You've always loved me."

From the corner of my eye, I could see Gabriel's

eyes blink open. There were holes in his shirt, but no blood. He was still alive.

I glared at Jacob so hard, I thought fire was going to shoot through my eyes.

"I've never loved you," I spat.

He took his gun in his hand and struck me hard against the side of the head, sending me back to my knees. Then, he grabbed me under the armpit and yanked me back up to face him.

"Say that again," he challenged, turning and pointing his gun at Gregory's face.

That was the final straw. There would be no more reasoning or begging with Jacob. He had already taken my husband and my sanity from me. If he thought for a moment that he was going to kill my son to get closer to me, he was dead wrong.

Without thinking, I rushed him, wrapping my arms around the back of his neck. I tried to pull him down from behind, but there was too big of a weight discrepancy between us. So, I held on for dear life as he swung me around like a rag doll, trying to get a good aim at my son and me.

"Gabriel!" I screamed, and it was as if my cries brought him back to life. Gingerly, the detective got to his feet and drew his weapon on Jacob.

"Stand back," Jacob said in a strangled voice as I put as much weight on the front of his throat as I could.

He aimed at Gabriel, but I tugged harder, causing him to miss his shot. Instead of hitting Gabriel, he shattered an overhead light, sending glass raining down upon us.

We were shrouded by darkness again, but the game had changed. It was three against one, and there was no way in hell I was going to lose this fight.

CHAPTER TWENTY-SEVEN

Jacob was strong, but there was no strength like a mother defending her innocent child. He dug his nubby fingernails into my hands, but I kept my grip around his neck, pushing my wrists into his trachea. Just like the leg wound, I was going to chip away at him until it was too much for him to survive. I couldn't deliver any big blows to him, but I could fight scrappy.

At one point, he nearly shook me off, but I recovered, knocking him off balance. He careened into the wall, holding his hands out in front of his face to take the brunt of the impact. In the process, the gun dropped from his hands onto the ground.

"Get it, Gregory," I shouted, but my son was understandably skittish. At some point in his early life,

I must have taught him to avoid guns at all costs. He walked a few steps forward but wouldn't touch it.

Jacob used this opportunity to dive to the ground, sending me sprawling next to him. I struggled beside him, reaching for the gun, but he was just so much bigger than me. My spirits plummeted as I saw his thick hand on top of the weapon. Another loss.

Desperate, I did the only thing I could do in that moment. So much rage and fear had built up inside me that I knew that I wanted to make him hurt as much as possible. If I had to die in that moment, I wanted to leave my mark. I jumped to my feet and kicked Jacob squarely in the groin with all the force I had. His body lurched forward in shock, and he dropped the gun again in the process. I dove forward, picked up the gun, and scrambled backward.

I felt a tremendous rush go through my body. I generally didn't like dealing with guns, but this felt good. I finally had leverage over the man who had terrorized me for so many years. Now, he was going to grovel at my feet for mercy.

The weapon felt heavy in my hand. I lightly rested my finger on the trigger. I knew that I was only supposed to do that when I was ready to fire, so I safely moved it back beside my other fingers.

I was not much of a gun enthusiast, but because Greg liked to shoot guns for sport, I accompanied him to the shooting range to see what it was all about. I figured if I at least tried it and didn't like it, I would be able to stay at home the next time he went out.

At the time, I didn't see what the allure was. I pinched the trigger and fired off a few shots at a target. I wasn't good, but I wasn't horrible either. If I needed to use a gun to protect myself, I was at least competent enough to hit my target.

Now, I felt something completely different. Even without using the gun, I was in control of the situation. With Gabriel standing behind me with his weapon drawn, we were unstoppable. Jacob took a few steps back and dropped to his knees, facing me. He was panting and red in the face, no doubt because of our scuffle. He looked so pathetic there, but I was out of compassion. He had done something so bad that I didn't think I'd ever fully recover.

"Annabeth, please," he whimpered.

I let out a dry laugh. "Save it," I said. "You threatened to kill me and my son. You shot a police officer. Do you think you're just going to get away with this?"

"I don't want violence," he said calmly.

"You should have thought about that a long time ago," I raged.

I heard my son clear his throat from behind me. I didn't want him to see his mother like this. I also wasn't done with Jacob. A better person would have walked away. I never claimed to be a better person.

He had already suffered enough. He didn't need to watch a grown man blubber for forgiveness and be arrested. I had a feeling he wouldn't go quietly, either.

"Can you take him somewhere?" I asked Gabriel, my voice soft and sorrowful. "I don't want him to see this."

"Why don't you take him up to my squad car?" Gabriel suggested. "You two can sit in the back and wait for backup to arrive. I can handle this if you can point the other officers in my direction when they get here."

"No," I replied firmly. "I'm going to stay here until it's over. I'm not going to let him chase me away. I'm going to stare into his eyes as he's carted to prison. I'm going to testify against him in court and tell the judge in great detail every way he's hurt my family. I'm going to ensure that he doesn't go free. I also don't want him to hurt you while I'm away. No, I'm not going to leave until this is over. If someone killed your wife and stole your kids and tried to keep you forever, what would you do? Would you let someone else put him in a police car, or would you deal with it yourself?"

Gabriel pursed his lips, but he didn't try to argue with me. He understood the hurt and rage I felt. I knew for a fact that Gabriel was the kind of guy who would make a sicko like this suffer if he had harmed his family.

"Gregory, sweetie, can you go up the stairs and wait in the police car until we're ready to go?" I asked my son. "I'll be right there. The adults have to talk first."

He stood firmly planted on the concrete floor. He didn't speak, but I could tell that he was frightened.

"It's okay, buddy," I said gently, all the while pointing the handgun at Jacob. "No one up there can hurt you. I promise it's safe."

He stayed mute. I sighed, knowing that it was of no use. I couldn't convince the kid to go up the stairs by himself and sit in a police car alone, especially after everything he'd been through. Still, I couldn't have him in the maze with me. I needed to tell Jacob a few things before our conversations would become documented by police and lawyers. If Gabriel would allow it, I had a few swift kicks to the crotch left in me too.

"Can you take him up there?" I asked Gabriel.

"I'm not going to leave you down here with this guy," he said exasperatedly.

"Why not? Afraid I'm going to kill him?"

"No. I don't really care if you kill him. It's my job to get him to the police station in one piece, but accidents happen. I don't want you to be here alone with him. I would never forgive myself if something happened to you."

A smile came to my lips. It was good to finally have someone on my side.

"What if you just ran him up the stairs to show him that it's safe? You can come right back down and cuff him, if that's what you want."

He gritted his teeth. "Fine. I swear, if I come back and you've done anything to hurt her, you will pay," he said, pointing his finger at Jacob. "Come on, Gregory. I think I have some snacks in my car for you."

"Mom!" Gregory exclaimed as Gabriel tried to take him by the hand.

"It's okay, Gregory," I said. "He's a good guy. You can trust him. Please go to his car. I'll be right there."

Gregory relented and tucked his hand into Gabriel's as they left the maze. My heart fluttered a little seeing them together.

"Annabeth," Jacob said conspiratorially, his eyes wide. "There's still time. Why don't you let me go and we'll pretend like this never happened? I'd be willing to let you go if you show me some mercy right now."

I furrowed my brow. "Why the hell would I do that?"

"Don't you remember what it was like in the old days? You were my best friend."

"I was a child. I didn't know any better."

"You liked me. We were so good together. I know I've gotten angry at you today and I hurt you. But I only did that because I love you and want what's best for you."

"Greg was best for me," I spat. "If you had only realized that, you would have never killed him. You ruined my life because it didn't include you. If you really loved me, you would have let me go. You only loved yourself."

"Your son needs a father. You're depriving him of a strong male role model. I want to be there for you."

"He had a father, and it was never you. Maybe one day, he'll have a new dad, but it will never be you. You're sick. I'd say you need help, but I know you don't want to change. You only want to manipulate others to get your way."

Jacob stared at me as if he were trying to read my mind. A normal person would have a look of remorse plastered all over their face. After all, I could end his life in a single shot and I'd be called a hero. There was no emotion behind his eyes. If anything, he had a look of contempt on his face. The words that came out of his mouth were apologetic. His facial expressions told a different story.

"I was once a boy, too, you know," he said. "I had dreams of owning my own business and working with computers. I only ever wanted to make a lot of money so I could have a beautiful wife who chose me over every other man out there. I wanted kids who doted after me. I wanted to be able to look at all the people I grew up with and laugh in their faces when they were getting divorced and their kids were knocked up or addicted to drugs. I wanted a lot out of life."

"You wanted a trophy family," I retorted. "Did you ever stop to think that if you were a good person, girls would like you?"

He laughed in my face. "Of course you would say that. You're no different from any of the stupid girls out there. Did you like me when we were young?"

"As a friend, yeah," I responded, my hand shaking now.

"So you thought I was a nice enough guy? Even earlier this week, you said that I was good to talk to and you were glad to have me around."

"So?" I said. "That's before I knew what you had done."

"That doesn't matter," he said, talking rapidly now. "If you thought I was such a good guy, why did you go for a meathead like Greg? Face it, girls don't like nice guys. They like guys who are rude to them because it makes things exciting. They like stereotypical guys with big muscles and pretty blue eyes. They like guys who will stick their cock in anything that moves."

"Don't you dare talk about Greg," I warned. "He was a really good guy."

"I was a good guy," he whined, his voice going up an octave. "I tried to give you everything, but you didn't want it. Every girl says they want a guy to treat her right, and every girl is a liar. You're the worst kind of liar because you give men like me hope that you will love us one day if we put in the work."

My mouth gaped open. I had never heard such entitlement come out of anyone, let alone someone I had known half of my life.

"So I'm a whore for choosing my own happiness over yours?" I asked, a maniacal smile appearing on my face.

"Finally, you're starting to see reason," he sighed. "I knew it was only a matter of time before you came around. See, females rarely listen to men. They think that they know what's best, but they do better when they have someone in charge of them. Look at you, Annabeth. You're a single mom who still lives at home. You deserve better. I could give you a house and help with the boy. You can work if you need something to keep you occupied during the day, but if you wanted to sit on the patio and eat bonbons all day, that would be fine with me. I'd dress you in the most beautiful clothes and put diamonds on your fingers. Greg didn't have enough money to treat you like the princess you are.

I'm running my own construction company and I'm selling my software to wealthy developers. I've got everything you could ever want. You just need to put the gun down and call off your dogs."

I scoffed. "Wow. You really think that I'm going to tell the police that I made a mistake? You think that I wouldn't press charges on you? You're delusional."

"And you're hysterical," he said.

"How could you kill my husband?"

He shrugged. "He was keeping us apart."

"How could you kidnap my son and stab my brother?"

"Your brother was collateral damage. I didn't feel the need to kill him, but he was in my way. Your son was the only way I knew to truly get to you. I kept him alive," he said, as though it was some favor to me.

"You beat me, starved me, held me hostage, and had your way with me," I said. "You don't do that to people you love. Explain that. "

He shrugged. "Trial and error. The amnesia was a nice benefit. I'd planted a seed that would cause you to come crawling back to me one day. I knew your subconscious would remember my touch and bring you back. I was right."

"How?"

"I didn't even have to call you today when I wanted to be around you. You just showed up right in front of me. Isn't that enough for you to settle down and forget all about this?"

"No," I replied, taking a step closer. "Not even close."

I looked back at the stairs, hoping to see Detective Reyes standing behind me. I was mentally drained and not sure if I could hold a discussion with Jacob for much longer. He stared at me with a smug smile on his face, as if he knew he was breaking me down.

"Tell me you love me," he said, licking his lips. "You're so sexy when you're scared. Ever since the day we met, I've been dreaming about the moment when you get into bed with me."

I heard Gabriel come back down the stairs over the pounding of my pulse in my ears.

"You're never going to hurt me again," I shouted.

"Baby, you live for this. You love being the damsel in distress. Just let your prince charming pick you up and carry you away."

I had heard enough. He reached his hand out to me and I pulled the trigger, shooting him squarely between the eyes. He fell onto his back, a broken man.

Gabriel rushed up to me and grabbed my shoulders from behind. I had just murdered a man. I didn't feel any remorse, just relief. I'd let him throw me in jail, knowing that I had removed a threat from the world.

"Are you okay?" he asked frantically, looking me over.

"I'm fine," I said calmly, my eyes closed. I didn't want to look at Jacob anymore.

He walked toward Jacob and pressed two fingers on his fat neck to check for a pulse, though it was quite evident that he could not be revived.

"The other car is here. They're going to take you and your son to the station. Do you need to go to the hospital?"

I shook my head.

"Good," he said, wrapping his arms around me, much to my surprise. I lingered in his arms for a moment, inhaling deeply. For the first time in recent memory, physical contact wasn't causing me to flinch or pull away.

"You're in for a long evening of questioning," he said morosely. "Hang in there, and I'll do my best to get you out so you can be with your son."

"How much trouble am I going to be in?" I asked, unable to meet his kind eyes.

He frowned. "None at all. But, it might help to use the words 'self-defense' when they ask about this part," he said, gesturing toward Jacob. "When they hear what he did to you and your family, they'll just wish that they could have shot the bastard sooner. Now, go upstairs and give your son a hug. He's very worried about you."

I walked up the long staircase without looking back at the subterranean maze and crawled into the backseat of the police car beside my son. I pulled him into my arms and planted a big kiss on the top of his head.

"Ready to get out of here?" the officer said to me, looking through his rearview mirror.

"You have no idea," I replied wearily, clutching my son close to my chest.

CHAPTER TWENTY-EIGHT

"So, are we still having nightmares?" Dr. Andrews asked as I sat next to Gregory on her couch.

"No," he replied simply as he twisted a Rubik's Cube. He had been quite cooperative in therapy this week, especially if he could keep his hands busy as he spoke to Gloria.

"That's great!" she exclaimed.

"I know," I replied, a smile on my face. "I haven't heard him wake up in the middle of the night for the past two nights.

"How about you?" she asked, directing her questioning toward me.

I sighed. "I'm still having nightmares. It's always similar to the ones I talked about in our session," I said cryptically, not wanting my son to hear what I had been dreaming of when I fell asleep beside him.

The nightmares were always the same. I'd find myself locked in the maze with Jacob while he was abusing me. In some dreams, Gregory would be standing a few feet away, just watching as Jacob performed unspeakable acts. Gloria suggested that I was worried about his innocence being taken. I had to agree with her assessment.

Dr. Andrews was constantly reminding me how resilient children were. Though my son had his own unique traits, the way his brain worked seemed to make no difference in how he processed trauma. He would certainly be affected by his kidnapping, but with regular therapy, Dr. Andrews believed that he would be able to live a normal life. And it appeared that he was already recovering, less than two weeks after the whole ordeal.

"I haven't taken any sleeping pills since Sunday," I added, trying to create a positive spin for myself. I needed all the victories I could get.

"That's good." She smiled. "You're finding that it's easier to fall asleep initially and go back to sleep after a nightmare?"

I nodded. "I'm still not sleeping through the night, but I'm less worried that I'm in danger. Sometimes, I'll get up and check the alarms and sensors to make sure they're working, but then I'll remind myself that he's dead and he can't hurt us anymore."

"And that's exactly what you should be telling yourself," she replied. "I must say, the two of you have made great strides. You should be proud of yourselves."

"We couldn't have done it without you," I said gratefully. "If we hadn't tried hypnotherapy, we might still be looking for him. Or, things could have been a lot worse for us."

"Oh, you did all the hard work," she said. "I just tried to guide you through. Well, we're all done for today. Will we see you on Friday?"

"We'll be here." I smiled, resting my hand on Gregory's head. I ruffled his hair, even though he didn't like it when I did so.

After therapy, I took Gregory to my mom's house for dinner. She met him at the door with a hug. Much to my surprise, he accepted it.

"How did it go?" she asked as I walked into the kitchen and set his backpack on the table.

"Really well," I replied. "I'm really proud of him."

"Me too," she said warmly. "I know it's been tough for him, but I think he's really growing up. He's not a little baby anymore."

"That's what I was afraid of," I groaned.

My mom put her hand on my shoulder. "I think he'll be just fine."

"I hope so. Does Tom still plan on coming to my place tomorrow?"

"Yes, he's being discharged at two. Can you still pick him up? I'm working."

"Yeah, just double-checking," I replied. I'm going to have to take some boxes out of the spare room before then."

"You're still not unpacked?" my mom asked, a look of surprise on her face.

"I haven't had a lot of time." I laughed. "I started with all of Gregory's stuff, but I haven't had the chance to dig through my stuff yet. I keep thinking I have more time before Tom gets out of the hospital."

"Do you want him to come here instead?" she asked, arching her brows.

"No," I protested. "We already decided that it was best if he stayed with us for at least a few weeks. Besides, you have to work. I can work and keep an eye on him. It's better this way."

"If you're sure," she said. "It's so quiet here without you."

"Well, you can have this kid as much as you want," I said, nodding toward Gregory, who was running laps around the living room. "He's all yours."

"Good." She smiled. "Now, are you going to take your jacket off and stay a while?"

I looked at my watch. "I'll be back before you sit

down for supper," I said. "I have to run to the police station."

"What now?" she groaned.

"Nothing," I said reassuringly. "I just have to sign a few statements. Apparently, I forgot to the last time I was there."

"Well, be quick. The casserole will be ready in twenty-two minutes."

"Got it," I said before dashing out of the house.

As I made my way to the police station, I found myself hoping that Gabriel hadn't gone home for the day yet. Out of all the police officers, he was by far my favorite. He was one of the few who made me feel like he actually gave a crap about my concerns. The others were diligent in their questioning, but they didn't have the same warmth that Gabriel had.

I even had a word with the police captain about how he had downgraded my case right before I was taken to the maze. He was very apologetic, but he didn't seem sincere. Afterward, I simply told him that it was important to take child kidnapping cases more seriously, and if it hadn't been for Gabriel, we would both be dead. It was hard to be calm and reasonable when I spoke to him, because all I wanted to do was scream in his face for nearly losing my son forever. But in the end, I think I got my point across rather nicely. If not, then the community members who wrote to him after my story was printed in the newspaper helped drive that point home.

Luckily, Gabriel's face was the first one I saw when I walked into the station. He looked surprised to see me. I found it rather charming. I think he was a few years younger than me, but he had the boyish charm of a guy fresh out of college. Even though his life hadn't been easy, he still had the attitude of someone whose work had yet to break him down. A lot of the officers seemed jaded and uninterested, but he took every little piece of information to heart, no matter how trivial they seemed. I hoped he'd always be that way.

"Oh, you're here for that paperwork," he said, smacking his palm to his face. "I totally forgot. It's been a long day."

"Did you get a new case?" I asked.

"I've got a couple. That's not the issue, though. I just got a call from my daughter's daycare. Apparently, there's been a lice outbreak and there's a chance she might have it. I was running out to get shampoo and a comb before picking her up. I've never dealt with this before."

"I'm sorry." I giggled. "I've been there before. Don't forget to wash all of your clothes and linens in hot water. I guess I'll have one of the officers guide me through whatever it is I need to do."

"No, I'll do it," he said hastily, guiding me toward

his office. "The paperwork is in here, anyway. Just sign your name next to the tags. You can read it if you want, but it's just your words."

"Cool," I said, scribbling my name on each page.

"Is your brother home?" he asked.

"Tomorrow," I answered. "He's doing so much better, and he's so eager to get out of the hospital. Gregory's doing really well, too. His therapist is impressed by how well he's doing."

"That's good to hear. I've seen people who have wounds like his, and a lot of times, it takes months until they're functional again. And you have such a good son. I remember your saying that he doesn't talk much, but I looked at one of his interview tapes and he was chattering away."

I laughed. "He was happy because you guys got him chicken strips and soda. And he likes talking about puzzles, and the maze was kind of like a puzzle to him."

"Well, I certainly learned a lot from him. So, how are you doing?"

"Fine," I said, a smile on my face, though it didn't quite feel genuine. "I'm hanging in there, at least."

"That's more than anyone could expect of you," he said earnestly. He lifted his hand like he was going to rest it on my shoulder, but he quickly dropped it back to his side. "Well, that's all I have for you now," he said, shuffling the papers back into his file folder. I'm sure someone's talked to you about civil suits—"

"I don't know," I groaned. "His parents used to live next door. They're good people and I don't want their money. It's not their fault he turned out so bad. And actually, they offered me a good chunk of his money because they felt so bad. But I feel weird about gaining from his money. I'm doing okay on my own. If anything, I'll just set up a college account or trust fund for my son and call it good. The less I have to think about him, the better."

"That's very noble of you," he said. "I don't know if I could say no to that money if I were in that situation."

"Maybe I'll tell his parents to make a donation to the police department. Maybe then your colleagues will take more interest in a Special Victims Unit."

"That could be useful." He sighed. "Well, it's been a crazy few weeks, hasn't it? I feel weird that I won't be seeing you regularly, but I guess that's a good thing, right?"

"I suppose so." I chuckled. "I hope I never have to return to a police station ever again, no offense."

He laughed. "None taken."

"You should probably go home," I said. "It sounds like you've got your work cut out for you."

"It's always something with two little girls in the house, that's for sure."

He walked with me through the station and to the parking lot. I gave him an awkward wave and unlocked my car.

"Wait," he said, rushing over to me. "I don't think there's a way to do this that isn't totally inappropriate, but I was wondering if you'd want to go out sometime, like for coffee or lunch or something. I know that you probably don't want to right now, but—"

"I've got your number, Detective," I said wryly. "I think we've both got a lot going on at home right now, but if things ever slow down, I might give you a call. Just promise me you won't wait by your phone. I don't do well with desperate types."

"Of course." He grinned. "Have a good evening, Ms. Simmons."

I got into my car and waited until he was a safe distance away before breaking out into giggles. I wasn't looking to get into a relationship, but it was such a relief that the guy who was into me was actually a good person. It was as good as it got after a decade of torture.

ABOUT COLE BAXTER

Cole Baxter loves writing psychological suspense thrillers. It's all about that last reveal that he loves shocking readers with.

He grew up in New York, where there crime was all around. He decided to turn that into something positive with his fiction.

His stories will have you reading through the night—they are very addictive!

Sign up for Cole's VIP Reader Club and find out about his latest releases, giveaways, and more. Click here!

For more information, be sure to check out the links below!
colebaxterauthor@gmail.com

ALSO BY COLE BAXTER

Stolen Son

Made in the USA
Coppell, TX
29 May 2020